DANNY ORLIS

and

KENT'S ENCOUNTER WITH THE LAW

BE

MOODY PRESS

CHICAGO

Contents

1

Jack on the Spot

SPRING WITH ALL ITS BEAUTY had arrived in Northern Minnesota. Grass and flowers, encouraged by a gentle sun, grew in wild profusion. The wind was on its best behavior and the lakes lay like jewels in their settings of green.

But Jack Ross was not thinking about the beauty around him. Not with a letter from Riley in his hand.

He hadn't realized that the color had fled from his face, or that his hands were trembling until his mother spoke.

"Jack," she said, her voice edged with concern, "what's the matter?"

"Nothin'." He scowled at her. "Nothin' at all."

"You act as though something terrible has happened," she continued.

"Aw, mom, that's just your imagination. There's nothin' wrong. I wish you'd lay off of me for once."

She came up to him. "Jack, who is your letter from?"

He jerked it away. "It's from a friend of mine. That's all."

"I didn't know you were acquainted with anyone in Chicago," she persisted.

Disgust gleamed in his sullen eyes.

"This guy doesn't actually live in Chicago. He just happens to be there for a couple of weeks. For cryin' out loud, Mom. Can't I even get a letter from somebody without gettin' the third degree?"

She laid her hand on his arm.

"I've been so worried about you lately, Jack." Her voice trembled. "You've acted so strange the last few weeks. Not like yourself at all. I can't help wondering if you're in some sort of trouble or something."

His youthful cheeks flushed.

"Mom, I wish you'd quit worryin' about me. I'm not in any trouble and I'm not about to get in any trouble. So quit gettin' so shook up about me."

"But you've been staying out so late at night for the past month or so."

He shook his head.

"How many times do I have to tell you that I'm not your little boy anymore. The other guys get to go out at night without having to take a lie detector test. Lay off, will you?" With that he stormed out the door. He didn't know what was the matter with his mom, anyway. She acted as though he was a little kid or something. Like he couldn't take care of himself.

Jack wanted to open this letter from Riley and read it immediately, but he didn't dare to with his mother in the mood she was in. There was no telling when she would come flying out of the house and jerk it out of his hands before he got a chance to put it away. Then he would be in real trouble.

Jack got in his car and drove down to the drugstore where he parked and opened the letter.

". . . Things have been looking up for me here," Jack read. "Picked up a bundle at the races last week." Jack grinned as he read. That Riley sure knew the angles. Probably got in on a deal to "fix" a horse race or two. He was that lucky. "I've made arrangements to move some more merchandise—all we can deliver. Fact is, those fellows'll pay a premium if they can get good stuff. I think it's time for us to set up operations again. I'll meet you at the usual spot, the same time, Saturday night." At the close of the letter was printed a warning: "Burn this immediately."

Jack crumpled the letter in his fist and drew in a long, deep breath. That was just what he was afraid of. Riley wanted him and the boys to go to work again.

Well, he wasn't going to do it! That was all there was to it. It was too risky. They'd almost gotten themselves caught the last time. Riley didn't need to think he could tell him what to do!

Jack was still sitting there when Linda Penner sauntered by. Impulsively he rolled down the window.

"Hi."

Her smile was warm and friendly.

"Hello, Jack. What're you doing all alone?"

"Waiting for you." He slipped the key from the ignition and got out. "How about some ice cream or something cold to drink?"

She hesitated.

"Or doesn't your 'watchdog' want you to be with me?" Jack continued.

Linda colored delicately. "Jack, please don't say things like that."

"Well, it's the truth, isn't it?" He took her arm and guided her toward the corner drugstore. "Doesn't that new wife of your dad's have orders to keep you away from me?"

"Nobody has given Elsie any orders about keeping us apart. I can tell you that much," Linda declared.

"But she does kick up a storm if she finds out that we've even seen each other. Isn't that a fact?" Jack sneered.

It was true that Linda's stepmother had talked with her about not going with unsaved fellows, and she had been furious about it, but hearing Jack criticize her was too much.

"Elsie is a lovely Christian woman and she treats me as well as any mother could treat a daughter." Linda was surprised at the vehemence in her voice. "And I don't like to hear you talk about her that way."

"OK, OK. We'll forget about your stepmother. How's that?"

He guided her to a back booth where they sat down across from each other. A waitress came up and took their orders.

"It's been a long time since we've even had a coke together."

"I—I've been busy," Linda retorted lamely.

"I know." His grin was taunting. "I know how busy you've been."

"If you don't believe me," she bristled, "you don't have to."

He leaned forward and patted her arm.

"Know something, kitten? I like to see you get mad that way. When you do, the sparks just fly."

"That's not very complimentary," she pouted.

"Why not? It's the truth." Just being with Linda made him feel better already. Riley was all but forgotten, at least for the moment.

Half an hour later Linda looked at her watch.

"Oh, Jack!" she exclaimed. "I had no idea it was so late. I've got to run."

"If you can wait long enough for me to pay the check I'll give you a ride home."

She shook her head quickly. "No, thanks."

His eyes searched hers questioningly. "What's the matter? Are you afraid to ride with me?"

"You know better than that," Linda said.

"Or is it the watchdog you're afraid of?" Jack sneered.

Linda's young mouth tightened. "Jack Ross! You make me so mad!"

"I'm sorry," he replied, laughing. "You have my apology."

Jack stood at the cashier's counter and watched Linda flounce outside. Her temper didn't bother him any. It was all a show. She'd be there when he wanted her. A crooked grin lifted one corner of his mouth. He couldn't quite figure her out. One minute she was as religious as a preacher and the next she was dancing with him at some out-of-the-way night spot. She could be so afraid of that stupid stepmother one time that she wouldn't even get in the car with him. The next, she didn't care who saw them and would sit there, laughing, while he pushed the accelerator to the floorboard.

If she was in the right mood she just might go for that deal of Riley's herself. She had the nerve.

He paid the check, pocketing his change without looking at it.

* * *

Jack waited impatiently for Saturday night and Riley. It seemed that the days would never pass.

The worst of it was he couldn't say anything to anybody about it. He just had to wait and worry about what was going to happen.

At last Saturday night came. Jack rode around aimlessly until almost time for the meeting. Then he turned north on the highway and tooled out of town toward the beer joint where they'd been meeting.

He slowed as he approached and was about to turn in when he remembered something Riley had told him. "Always 'case' a place first. Go by with feigned indifference so as to size up the situation and check to see that there aren't any visitors you don't want to see you."

Jack's stomach tightened convulsively.

Slowly he drove past the poorly lighted tavern, his eyes searching the parking lot for a familiar car. His breath was coming in short, quick stabs and his hands trembled on the wheel. Strange, but he'd never known fear like this before he met Riley and started doing his dirty work.

A highway patrolman went by and it was all Jack could do to keep from floorboarding his hot rod to get out of there. And he hadn't been doing a thing except drive along at about half the speed limit. The officer hadn't even given him a second look.

That decided it! No sir! He didn't care how Riley stormed. He was through with that business! He wasn't going to spend the rest of his life being afraid of his own shadow.

When he drove into the tavern parking lot some minutes later he saw no sign of the man he was supposed to meet. In spite of himself, his spirits rose. Perhaps Riley had changed his mind about coming. Perhaps he had gone somewhere else. Perhaps he hit it real good at the races a couple more times and figured that was better than—that— He swallowed against the knot in his throat.

He'd wait a couple of minutes more and then go back to town. Just long enough so he could tell Riley, if he ever saw him again, that he had kept his part of the bargain.

Jack was reaching down to turn the ignition key and start the engine when a dark figure materialized out of the shadows. Jack's blood iced. He didn't need to see the man's face. He already knew who it was.

Riley opened the car door and slid onto the seat beside him.

"Hi, Jack." He smiled evilly. "How're things going?"

"OK," Jack retorted lamely.

"We'd better get out of here. The place is really jumpin' with people tonight."

Mechanically Jack started his car and backed out of the parking stall.

"Better take it easy, Jack." There was fear in the man's voice. "There's a car coming in. Don't pull out far enough so their headlights shine on us."

"OK."

Riley scooted down in the seat until he couldn't be seen even if the lights did catch them. But he needn't have worried. Jack was an old hand at this sort of thing. He should be. He'd had plenty of practice dodging people when he'd taken Linda out. He hung back until the car had entered the parking lot. Even then he waited momentarily, until the car was even with the first row of parked cars. When Jack moved forward, the line of vehicles was between him and the strange automobile.

Not until they were out on the highway did his passenger speak.

"Say," Riley exclaimed admiringly, "you handled that like a veteran. You're goin' to be all right."

Jack grunted something or other.

"Well, I'm sure glad you showed up tonight. We've got to get your guys together and get set up. We've got a lot of work to do to give these new contacts of mine all the stuff they need."

The boy did not speak.

"Did you tell anybody I was comin'?"

"Nope."

"That's the stuff. It's best that nobody knows I'm here. I'll get me a room in one of the motels on the edge of town and stay out of sight until we're ready to go."

Jack glanced at his companion uneasily.

"Everything's been quiet around here, hasn't it?" Riley asked presently.

"I guess so."

The man straightened and his face grew harsh.

"What's the trouble with you, anyway?" he demanded. "Are you scared or somethin'?"

"No!" Jack blurted. "I ain't scared."

"Then what's eatin' you? You act as though you've just been invited to a hangin'."

The youthful driver cleared his throat.

"I'd just as well tell you, Riley. I ain't goin' to help you no more."

"What?" The man's voice was ice. "What did you say?"

"I said I ain't helpin' you no more."

It was a full minute before Riley spoke again. When he did, rage trembled in his voice.

"You listen to me, Jack Ross! And listen to me good! You ain't goin' to back out on nobody. Understand?"

"I can if I want to," Jack blurted.

"I been patient with you, Ross! I've taught you everything you need to know to keep you from gettin' caught. I've bought the stuff you stole and paid you good prices for it. No questions asked. I even advanced you money when you was broke." He grabbed Jack by the arm and squeezed so hard the boy cried out. "But I never done it so you could quit on me just when I needed you! Don't you forget it!"

"It ain't that I don't appreciate what you've done for me, Riley." Jack moistened his lips nervously.

"But I just don't want to get into no trouble with no cops."

"How many times do I have to tell you that we aren't goin' to have any trouble with the cops. That is, of course, unless you go ahead with that stupid idea of yours of quittin'. If you do that, I'll see that the sheriff finds out everything he needs to know to put you in the reformatory for one to five."

Jack hesitated.

"You—you wouldn't dare do that," he stammered. "You'd be gettin' yourself in trouble too."

The man laughed archly. "You just leave that to me. There's ways of doin' most anything you set your mind to." He paused and took a deep breath. "I don't blame you for gettin' the jitters once in awhile. I do, myself, between jobs. But don't let this get you all shook up, Jack. We've got a good thing goin' for you and me. Don't spoil it."

"But—"

"Don't give it another thought. I'll take care of everything." He laughed again. "The cops didn't even come close to catchin' us the other times, did they?"

"I—I guess not," Jack said reluctantly.

"And they're not goin' to come close this time either. I tell you, this is a snap, Jack. There's no other way I know of that a fella your age can earn the kind of money I've been givin' you. Now, is there?"

Jack turned at the next side road, and slowed to a crawl.

"I—I—"

"You just leave everything to me. Get your guys together and I'll do the rest."

"And if I don't?"

Their eyes met briefly.

"You will!" Riley swore for emphasis. "If you know what's good for you, you will!"

2

Kent Agrees

For the space of a minute or more
Jack stared at Riley. The boy's breath came in short,
quick stabs and terror filled his eyes.

"Now I don't want to have no more trouble with
you, Jack. OK?"

"I'm afraid my folks are gettin' onto me," he protested weakly. "You should've heard my mom when
your letter came the other day. She gave me the
third degree."

Riley shrugged his protests away. "We don't have
anything to worry about on that score. You've been
lyin' to her for the past ten years. You surely can
think of somethin' to tell her that'll take her off our
backs."

"But—"

Riley's voice grew cold and ominous. "Don't make
me mad, Jack. I'm givin' you fair warning." His

manner changed. "Relax, fella. All I want you to do is help with one more job."

"One more?"

"That's what I said." Riley nodded.

"And if I help, you won't try to make me help you anymore. Is that right?"

"That's a promise."

Jack sighed deeply.

"I'll help you just this once, Riley. But that's got to be the end of it. When that's over I'm through."

"Sure—sure— Now this is what I want you to do. Get hold of your guys and get them together for the day after tomorrow."

Jack gasped. "So soon?"

"I told you everything was all set." Impatience edged Riley's voice. "We've got to move and move fast."

Jack eyed him uncertainly.

"I don't plan on backing out of the deal." He spoke slowly. "But I—I don't know whether I can even get the guys together that soon. It takes time in order to work with them."

Once more the man's hand snaked out and grasped Jack savagely by the wrist.

"I said I wanted those kids for day after tomorrow, Ross. And that's when I'm goin' to have them. If they aren't there you've got to answer to me!"

Jack pulled away and rubbed his wrist. "If I can't

get them I—I just can't get them. That's all there is
to it."

"That ain't good enough for me! If you know
what's good for you you'll have them at our meeting
place at eight o'clock sharp," Riley declared.

Jack swallowed hard. "So—so early?"

Riley nodded. "Don't ask me no questions now.
I'll fill you in when we're all together."

Jack did not reply.

"All you've got to do for now is get the kids together," Riley continued. "I'll take care of the rest."

"You—you don't need to worry about me. I'll get
'em," Jack said.

The older man nodded. "That's better." It was
some time before he spoke again. "You'd better take
me by the tavern now— Just remember what I told
you. Keep your mouth shut, but have them kids together."

"OK, OK," Jack retorted irritably. "You don't need
to get so shook up. I'll take care of everything."

He drove back to the tavern and let his companion
out of the car.

"Thanks, Ross."

"I'll be seein' you," Jack said.

Riley leaned forward and lowered his voice. "Need
any dough?"

Jack hesitated. "I guess not."

"I never saw a guy who couldn't use a little foldin'
money. Here. Take this and buy that girl of yours

a treat." He threw a ten-dollar bill on the seat and closed the door.

Jack looked down at the bill beside him. He could use it all right. The money they'd gotten from their earlier stealing escapades had long since been spent. It had come so easily that Jack had found it hard to go to work to get his spending money.

He should take the money back to Riley, or mail it to him and tell him he was having no part of him or his big deals. But he couldn't do that! A fellow just didn't double-cross a guy like Riley and get away with it. And he couldn't back out either. Not unless he wanted to go to jail. Riley wasn't lying. He'd do it.

It was better this way. He'd help Riley this one time, and he'd let him out. He picked up the bill and stuffed it into his pocket.

Jack didn't sleep much that night. However, he was up half an hour earlier the next morning. He drove around until he saw Kent Gilbert walking to school. Whipping around the corner, he stopped beside Kent and opened the car door.

"Hi, Kent."

The younger boy looked at him without speaking.

"Hi," Jack said again, motioning Kent toward the car.

Kent stood motionless on the sidewalk.

"Come on. I ain't got all day," Jack stated.

Kent shook his head. "I wish I could ride with you,

Jack, but I can't. Danny would clobber me if I did."

"Don't tell him."

"You don't know Danny. He finds out everything about everything." He shook his head. "I can't do it."

"He's not going to find out a thing about it," Jack went on. "And besides, there's nothin' he could do if he did. All you're doin' is riding to school with me. There ain't no law against that."

"There is in his book. He told me he'd skin me alive if he caught me with you—or even heard that I was with you." Kent's voice increased in volume, as though the very sound would persuade Jack he was telling the truth.

With that he started to walk along the sidewalk in the direction of the school. But Jack was not to be dissuaded so easily. He drove along beside him.

"Kent, I don't want to have to get mad. Come on over here and get in. I've got something I want to talk to you about."

"I don't want to talk to you."

Jack's face darkened. "I don't care what you want. You're goin' to come over here and get in! I've got to talk to you this morning!"

The younger boy hesitated, but only for an instant. With considerable reluctance he approached the car and got in.

"That's better," Jack said as he pulled away from

the curb. "You don't need to try to give me so much static. I just want to talk to you."

Kent nodded but his eyes were filled with fear.

Jack drove through town before he spoke again. "Well, Kent," he began at last. "The heat's off and we didn't get caught."

"We didn't get caught," Kent said, shuddering, "but, man, it was close. Every time I think of it I break out with goose bumps."

"I just wanted to tell you that we're gettin' together again tomorrow night."

Kent gasped. "No!"

"There's nothing to worry about," the older boy went on, hoping his own fear didn't show through. "There won't be any trouble."

The boy's lips narrowed slightly. "We—we aren't goin' to do nothin' more, are we?"

"Everything's planned. There won't be any sweat at all," Jack proceeded.

"Oh, no!" Kent retorted quickly. "You can count me out! I'm through!"

"There's nothing to it," Jack insisted.

"I don't care if there isn't. And I don't care what we're after. I ain't goin' to help steal so much as a stick of gum!"

Jack stopped the car and, leaning over the same way Riley had done to him, grasped his companion's wrist. "Now you listen to me, Kent Gilbert! You get that idea out of your head. You're in on this deal the same as the rest of us, and you're not quittin' now."

Kent's face paled. "I—I can quit if I want to," he stammered.

"Just try it!" Jack was whispering, but his voice was harsh with anger. "Just you try it and you'll wish you hadn't. Nobody quits on this deal!"

Kent tried to jerk away. "Take it easy, will you? That hurts."

"If you don't want to be hurt, quit this talk about gettin' out. That makes me mad. See?"

Kent swallowed hard. "I—I'd like to go along with you and the guys, Jack, but I can't do it anymore." His voice quavered and, once or twice, failed him. "I tell you, Danny and Kay are watchin' me so close I can't get away from them at night. They won't even let me out of the house to go to the library to study. No matter how hard I tried I wouldn't be able to get out and do nothin'."

Jack smiled slightly. "I was talkin' to Riley the other night. He's the fella who's been buyin' our stuff."

Kent nodded.

"When him and me decided on this job he said I should come around and see you guys. He said if anybody tried to quit, I was to let him know. He'd handle the quitter personally."

Kent sucked in his breath. "Wh-wh-what did he mean by that?"

"Just what do you think he meant?"

Kent licked his dry lips nervously.

"He's big and tough," Jack went on. "You can tangle with him if you want to. But if I were you I believe I'd do what he said."

There was a brief silence.

"Now, do you want me to tell George Riley you're chickening out on us?" Jack threatened.

The boy's reply was quick and filled with fear.

"I—I didn't say that," he protested. "I just said that it was going to be hard for me to get out and—and that I might not be able to get out all the time. I—I just wanted you to understand. That's all."

"Well now, that's better. That's much better." Relief was evident in Jack's voice and he grinned widely. "I thought you'd come around. I'll see you tomorrow night at the same place and give you the scoop."

"But I—I don't know whether I can get out of the house or not," Kent Gilbert continued. "Danny hardly lets me go from one room to the other without reporting to him and getting his permission."

Jack leaned forward.

"Listen, Buster! You'd better get out of that house tomorrow night. That's all I can say! If you don't, you'll have to answer to Riley!"

Kent left Jack's car and walked hesitantly up the school steps. A couple of kids spoke to him, but he did not reply. He was in for it now! He didn't dare turn Jack and Riley down. Not with that big, ugly character around to—to pulverize him. And if he went along with the gang, they'd probably get caught and he'd end up in jail. His thin young shoulders trembled, and the sweat came out on his face. How did a guy get into a mess like this anyway?

3

Linda Involved

Jack WAS AS RELUCTANT as Kent had
been to go through with their plans to help Riley.
He was greatly relieved when the older man got in
touch with him and postponed the meeting.

"Something has come up that I've got to go out of
town to take care of, Jack," he said. "We'll have to
hold everything until I get back."

Concern leaped to the boy's eyes.

"You aren't in some kind of trouble, are you?" he
asked. "It isn't because the cops are onto you—is
it?"

Riley snorted his disdain. "The cops! That's all
I've heard out of you lately. You're scared of the
cops! If you keep that up you'll do something to
give us away for sure."

"I ain't goin' to give nobody away," Jack protested, but without enthusiasm.

"This is just something that's got to be taken care of," Riley continued. "I'll be gettin' in touch with you as soon as I'm back."

"OK. I'll tell the guys."

"You do that. And don't forget to tell 'em that this doesn't change a thing. All that's different is the date." He paused momentarily. "If I were you I'd start cultivatin' that gal of yours again. I still think she'll give you the best alibi you could have."

"I don't know whether she'll even go out with me or not," Jack said hesitantly. "I've been talkin' to her, but she doesn't act as though she's going to."

Riley flashed a brief smile. "Turn on the old charm. She'll be eating out of your hand by the time we're ready to go."

Jack tried to see Linda that night, but she was nowhere around. He debated calling her at the house, but decided against it. After all, that would just cause trouble and wouldn't accomplish anything. It would be better to catch her at school or uptown.

The following morning Jack saw Linda in the halls, but there was only time to make arrangements to meet her later.

"I've got something terribly important to talk to you about."

"Well—" she hesitated. "I could only see you for a couple of minutes. I've got a lot of studying to do tonight."

"This won't take long. How about meeting me out at my old jalopy as soon as school's out?"

"I won't be able to go riding with you."

Jack's temper flared. "How many times do I have to tell you that I only want to talk to you?"

Linda was out at the car that afternoon when Jack came hurrying up.

"Hi, kitten."

She glanced impatiently at her watch. "I really have to rush, Jack."

"Oh, for cryin' out loud! I just get here and you tell me you have to hurry. If you're that anxious to get away from me I'm sorry I bothered you."

Her manner changed slightly. "I'm not anxious to get away from you. I just want to get home so I can study."

He took a long, deep breath. "I don't suppose it'll do any good for me to ask you," he began. "You've been treating me like a wornout shoe the last few weeks, but, Linda, I—I think so much of you I've got to take a chance on your turning me down anyway."

Her cheeks paled slightly.

"W-w-would you go somewhere with me again?" Jack asked.

"I—I—" Her voice choked. "We went over all that a long time ago. Remember?"

Dejection clouded his eyes. It wasn't only the alibi he was thinking about. When it came to a date she was the greatest. She was game for anything. Or at least she had been before she went nuts on religion.

"I've tried dating other girls, but that's no good. If I can't go with you I don't care to go with anyone. That's all there is to it."

She laid a hand on his arm. "I wish it could be different, Jack. Honestly, I do."

His face lighted. "It can be. All you've got to do is start going with me again."

She was a long while in answering. "You know it isn't that simple."

His gaze met hers. "Does that religion of yours mean that much to you, Linda?"

"It means everything in the world to me."

He sighed. "You sure do make it sound wonderful. When you talk that way you almost make me wish I was a Christian."

"Oh, Jack! If you would only accept Christ as your Saviour everything would be straightened out between us. And you'd be so happy. I know you would."

He frowned thoughtfully. "There are so many things I don't understand about it."

Excitement gleamed in her eyes. "Why don't you go with me to see Pastor Reeves? He could answer your questions."

Jack shook his head. "I don't even know the guy."

"If you don't want to go and talk with him, Danny

would talk to you. Why don't we go and see if he's home?"

"Just hold your horses a little bit. I didn't say I wanted to talk to anyone. I just said I had some questions."

"Oh," Linda replied.

He studied her young face carefully. "I don't think I want to go and talk with anyone," he continued momentarily, "but I will do this. If you'll go out with me one night next week I'll go to church with you the following Sunday. How about it?"

"I—I'd like to, but—"

"It's up to you," he bristled. "Do you want me to go to church, or don't you?"

"You know I do," she countered.

"All right, then. Go with me next week. If you do I'll go to church with you the following Sunday."

She hesitated. "What night do you want me to go with you, Jack?"

"I'll have to let you know. I've got some things to do next week and I'm not sure just when I'll be free. But if you'll go with me somewhere, I'll go to church with you. Is that a deal?"

"I—I guess so."

His temper flared. "What do you mean, you guess so? Don't you know?"

"Yes," she told him. "I'll go with you. That is if you'll give me your word of honor that you'll go to church with me the very next Sunday."

He grinned. "That's great." His smile broadened. "That's just great. I'll be seein' you."

He stood beside his car watching as she walked away. He had done it just as Riley said he could. All he had had to do was turn on the old charm and Linda was putty in his hands. It looked as though everything was going to work out OK in the girl department. It'd be worth it, too, even though he might have to go to church once in awhile to keep Linda in line.

As Linda walked home she too was thinking about the conversation she had just had with Jack. She always had enjoyed going with Jack. He was different than the other fellows she had dated. Going with him was unpredictable and exciting. And now there was a chance that she could win him for Christ!

When she got home from school Elsie was there alone. Linda took her books into her bedroom and returned to the living room where she sat down across from her stepmother.

"Hello, Linda. I didn't hear you come in."

"I came in the back door."

Elsie put aside the magazine she had been reading. "You look as though you're carrying the weight of the whole world on your shoulders, my dear."

"There is something I—I'd like to have you pray about," the girl began.

"Yes?"

"I think I've got a chance to lead Jack to Christ."

Elsie did not answer immediately. She picked up the magazine once more, fingering it with nervous hands. "What makes you think that?"

"He's promised to go to church with me a week from Sunday night," Linda answered.

"I see," Elsie said.

"I was wondering if you would pray for him?" Excitement sparkled in Linda's eyes.

"Of course I'll pray for him, Linda," Elsie said gently. "As a matter of fact, your dad and I have been praying for him for quite awhile."

"Oh, I'm so excited I can hardly wait," Linda retorted, getting up and moving to another chair closer to her attractive stepmother. "If Jack would only accept Christ I think I'd be the happiest girl in the world."

Elsie chose her words carefully.

"I don't want you to think I'm overly suspicious, Linda," she began after a time, "but there's something that bothers me about all of this. How does it come that he's going to wait until Sunday after next to go to church? Why doesn't he go this Sunday?"

"Well—" Linda paused reluctantly.

The older woman waited.

"He—he wants me to go with him somewhere next week," she blurted at last.

"And in return for your going with him he's going to church. Is that it?"

Linda nodded. "But I know that if he gets to church he'll accept Christ as his Saviour. *I just know it.*"

For the space of a minute or two Elsie sat quietly. "I know how you feel about Jack," she began. "There was a young man in my own life one time who wasn't a Christian and I wanted so desperately to win him for Christ. But finally I saw that I was breaking a command of God's by dating Arnold, and I broke up with him."

"Did he ever become a Christian?" Linda questioned.

Elsie shook her head. "The last I heard of him he was running a dice game in one of the gambling casinos in Las Vegas. He divorced his wife and married one of the women who danced in the chorus there. So you see what I was spared by obeying God's word about being unequally yoked."

"But Jack is different," Linda countered. "I've talked and talked with him about Christ. He's interested now. I know he is. If he can just get to church a few times I know the Holy Spirit will work in his heart."

Elsie went over and put a hand on Linda's shoulder. "My dear, the Holy Spirit can work in Jack's life and heart without you."

Linda looked up appealingly. "I know that, but—"

"Your father doesn't want you to go with Jack, Linda." Elsie's voice grew stern.

"This is different," Linda declared. Impulsively she got to her feet and crossed the room. In spite of herself, her temper flared. "How is Jack going to be won for Christ if Christians won't have anything to do with him?"

Quietly Elsie answered her. "I'm sure there are plenty of Christian fellows who are trying to befriend him and witness to him, Linda. Perhaps Jim Morgan would try to get him to go to church with him."

"A lot of good that would do!" Linda's eyes blazed. "He feels the same about Jack as you and Daddy do. He wouldn't have anything to do with him."

"If he wouldn't, there are others."

Linda came back to stand before her belligerently.

"I don't know why you've got it in for Jack. You don't know him. You don't know what he's like."

"We know that he isn't a Christian," her stepmother went on. "And the Bible is very clear about Christians dating those who aren't saved."

"That does it!" Linda exclaimed. "You don't need to think you're going to tell me what to do! You're not my mother! You can't boss me around!" Her voice raised to a shout! "You'd just as well know it. I told Jack I was going with him and that's exactly what I'm going to do."

4

Chance Encounter

THE FOLLOWING EVENING Jack saw Riley unexpectedly and the man waved him down.

"Am I ever glad I saw you," Riley said as he crawled into the car beside Jack. "Go out to the country where we can talk."

Obediently Jack turned the corner and headed for the highway.

"Tomorrow night's the night," Riley began after several minutes.

"Tomorrow night?" Jack's eyes widened. "I thought you said it wouldn't be till next week."

Riley lit a cigar and blew a thin stream of smoke in the boy's direction. "What I said was that we were going to wait until I got back." His eyes narrowed significantly. "Well, I'm back."

"Is—is everything set?" Jack tried to act interested, but his voice faltered and his hands were moist with sweat.

"That's what I want to ask you," Riley replied.

"They're OK from this end," Jack responded.

"Good. We'll get together tomorrow night at the same time and place."

Jack nodded. "We'll be there."

❊   ❊   ❊

Jack half expected to have trouble with Linda when he saw her the next morning, but to his surprise she agreed readily. "Do you want me to stop by your house, or do you think it would be better to meet at the drugstore about seven-thirty tomorrow night?"

Linda lowered her voice. "It would never do for you to come to my house."

He laughed. "What's that stepmother of yours going to think when she finds out that you've been with me?"

Anger flamed in Linda's dark eyes. "I don't care what she thinks. She's not running my life!"

"That's the stuff! That's the way you used to talk! We'll show 'em that they can't shove you around!"

❊   ❊   ❊

When school was out that afternoon Jack drove slowly up one street and down another as though he was just riding around. However, there was method in his every move. He had to find the rest of his gang and get them out that night. By six o'clock he had seen all but Kent. He was beginning to get concerned, when he saw Kent come out of an alley and cross the street on his way to the Orlis home. He drove up and stopped beside him.

"Hi, Kent," he said, opening the door. "I've been looking all over for you."

Fright widened the younger boy's eyes and he glanced about wildly, as though undecided whether to stand there or run.

"I—I've got to get home or Danny'll be mad."

"Hop in. "I'll take you home."

"I—I can't do it. You don't know what Danny'd do to me if—if he ever saw me with you."

"He's not going to see us. Come on!"

Something about Jack's voice caused the younger boy to do as he was bidden. He got in the car, but sat as close to the door as he could. His gaze bored into the floor.

Jack turned at the next corner. "Well, Kent, how've things been going for you?"

"All right." His lips trembled. "At least they were goin' all right until you came along."

"Don't talk that way or you'll have me feeling bad." Jack grinned evilly. "After all I'm just going to help you make some easy money."

The Gilbert boy shook his head vigorously. "I aint' havin' nothing more to do with you, Jack, an' I don't want your money, or anything else from you."

Jack's mouth dropped to a hard, dark scowl. "Well,

you're stuck with me whether you want to be or not. And don't you forget that for a minute!"

There was a brief hesitation before Kent answered. "What d'you want me to do?"

"I've already told you. We need your help. And you're goin' to forget this idea of chickening out."

"I ain't chickened out on you, an' I ain't goin' to."

"You're sure of that, Kent?"

"That's what I said, ain't it?"

"That's better. That's a lot better." Jack turned again, slowing perceptibly. "Tonight's the night."

Kent Gilbert's face blanched.

"T-t-tonight?"

"That's right. You be at the meeting place at eight o'clock sharp."

"I—I don't think I can make it so early. I—I've got to wait until everybody else's in bed."

"I said for you to be there!" Jack's voice was a threat.

"B-b-but why so early?" Kent demanded. "Th-there's too many people around at that time of the evening. We'll be caught for sure."

"Nobody's goin' to get caught. How many times do I have to tell you that?"

Kent moistened his lips uneasily. He knew that his face was white. "What are we goin' to do?"

"We'll clue you in tonight."

Danny and Kay Orlis both saw that something was wrong with Kent when he sat at the table a few minutes later and only toyed with his food. "What's the matter, Kent? Don't you feel well?"

"There ain't nothin' wrong with me." There was a brief silence. "Tonight's prayer meeting, ain't it?"

"Wednesday night is always prayer meeting night."

Kent was studying his plate and fighting to control his voice. "Are—are we goin'?"

"Kent," Danny answered, "you know we always go to prayer meeting on Wednesday night." He paused thoughtfully. "Is there some special reason why you're so interested in prayer meeting all of a sudden?"

The boy shook his head vigorously. "Can't a fella ask a simple little question without gettin' the third degree?" He pushed back from the table and got to his feet. "I'm gettin' fed up with the way you treat me around here!"

Danny's gaze caught him and held him motionless.

"I think you'd better go to your room, Kent." He spoke quietly but with authority. "I'll be in and talk with you in a few minutes."

The rest of the meal was eaten in comparative silence. When they finished Danny went in and sat on a chair next to Kent's bed. For a long while he talked with the boy about his arrogance and his attitude toward authority and other people. He looked for another opportunity to present Christ to Kent, but it did not come. At last Danny got to his feet. "You know I've got to punish you, don't you, Kent?"

The boy rolled over and looked up at him. For an instant—but only for an instant—a softening light flickered in his eyes. A light that pleaded for help and understanding. Then his old defiance surged back.

"You usually do," he blurted.

"I'm going to insist that you come home right after school the next two nights, and that you stay home both evenings, including tonight after prayer meeting."

Kent shuddered as though Danny had slapped him across the mouth, and terror seemed to twist his face. He had to go out tonight. He just had to! Jack and Riley would get him if he didn't show up! He was trembling violently when Danny left the bedroom.

✻   ✻   ✻

That day after school Linda had gone directly home. She was almost there when Jack pulled up and beckoned her over to the car. Excitement flushed his young face.

"Hi, kitten. Still going to meet me at the drugstore tonight?"

"I said I'd be there, didn't I?"

"That you did. I was just checkin'."

"I'll be there at seven-thirty," she promised him.

He grinned at her crookedly. "Know something,

kitten? I figured that religion of yours would start to wear thin before long."

"It's not that," she said defensively. "It's only that— It's only that—" Her words trailed miserably away.

"Forget it. You're goin' with me. That's all that matters." Jack's voice raised insistently. "But don't forget, seven-thirty sharp!"

Until Linda had talked with Jack that morning she had been sure of exactly what she would do. She was going to show Elsie that she wasn't going to order her around. She'd do as she pleased. If she wanted to go with Jack, that's what she'd do. Nobody was going to stop her!

Now, however, doubts began to creep into her mind. What was that smart remark Jack had made about her religion? It had sounded as though he didn't respect her faith anymore now that she had finally consented to go with him.

Then there was the matter of talking back to Elsie. She had had no right to do that. Even though Elsie wasn't her real mother, she loved her and was as good to both her and Becky as their own mother could possibly have been. And she had their best interests at heart. Much as she hated to admit it Linda knew that that was true. She knew, as well, that that was the reason why her stepmother had forbidden her to go with Jack.

But something within her rebelled at the very

thought of taking orders from Elsie. In spite of her-self anger flamed in her cheeks.

When Linda entered the house that afternoon, Elsie spoke to her as warmly as though there had not been any words between them the day before. But not so with Linda. Her gaze met Elsie's, expression-less and hostile. She did not speak.

"Your dad called about noon," her stepmother told her. "He won't be home until tomorrow night."

"So?" Linda flounced into the other room and threw her books on the bed. She had to decide about Jack right away. What was she going to do?

5

Linda Reneges

AT SUPPERTIME Linda came out of her bedroom and ate. She went back in as soon as she had finished. There was some homework she had to have done for the next morning, especially if she went out with Jack that night, but her books lay unopened on the bed. It was seven o'clock now. In thirty minutes she was supposed to meet him. In anguish she sank to her knees and began to pray. "Dear God, what should I do? What should I do?"

She was on her knees when the answer came so clearly it was startling. Why pray for God's guidance about something, she reasoned, when she already knew that it was against His will?

Resolutely she got to her feet and went to the telephone, dialing Jack's number. His mother answered.

"I don't know where Jack is," she answered. Her voice was filled with concern. "He didn't come home

45

for dinner this evening. I don't know where he is."

Linda hesitated.

"I—I see—"

There was a long silence. Then Mrs. Ross asked, "Would you care to leave a message?"

"A message?" Linda echoed. "Oh—oh, no, thank you. I'll call later or—or see him somewhere."

Slowly she returned the phone to its cradle. Jack was already at the drugstore, or on his way there. That meant that he would be waiting for her. He'd be furious if she didn't show up. He would never go to church with her unless she kept her part of the bargain.

She went to the closet and reached for her sweater, but with her hand on the hanger she checked herself. If she went down to the drugstore to explain why she couldn't go with him, she might end up by letting him talk her into going out with him, after all. She did like Jack better than she wanted to admit it, even to herself. He could influence her in ways she didn't like to be influenced. She closed the closet door, and for a moment stood there, summoning strength and courage.

There was only one thing left for her to do.

Hesitantly she went into the kitchen where Elsie and Becky were finishing the dishes. Her stepmother smiled at her brightly.

"Hi, Linda. I thought you were studying."

"Not right yet." She spoke with great hesitance.

"I'd like to talk to you as soon as you're through."

"We've almost finished. I'll be with you in just a minute." Linda stood somberly by the door until her stepmother poured out the dish water and put the pan away. "Now, what can I help you with?"

Linda swallowed against the tightening in her throat. "Let's go in my room where we can talk."

She switched on the light and closed the door behind them. For the space of a minute or two neither spoke. At last Linda took half a step toward the older woman. The expression on her young face had changed.

"I—I want to tell you how sorry I am th-that I talked the way I did to you last night," she began.

Her stepmother smiled understandingly. "That's quite all right, Linda."

"No it isn't," the girl protested. "I don't have any right to fly at you the way I did." Tears came to her eyes. "I know that you only want to do what's best for me." Unashamedly she dabbed at her eyes. "And I know it isn't best for me to go with a boy like Jack."

She sank to the bed beside Elsie. "Will you forgive me?"

Her stepmother put her arm about her. "Of course, I will."

For several minutes Linda cried uncontrollably. When she could speak she raised her head. "I don't want to say things like that to you. Honestly, I don't. And I don't want to do things a Christian shouldn't.

But it seems I can't even do what I know is right."
Again her face clouded. "What's wrong with me
anyway?"

Elsie's smile was tender and understanding.

"Nothing is wrong with you. Nothing at all. The
Bible tells us that we are new creatures when we accept Christ as our Saviour, but we still have our old
natures. Satan wars against the Holy Spirit within us.
That's the reason it's so easy for us to do the things
that are wrong. Sometimes it's hard for us to do the
things we know we should."

Linda took a long while in answering. "I don't
want to be like I am," she said. "Will—will you pray
for me?"

"I always pray for you, honey. Every single day."

"I know that, but I was wondering if—if you'd pray
for me especially about this—this temper of mine
and—and that I can live the way a Christian should."

"Of course, I will." Elsie Penner was crying now,
silently, as they knelt together.

They had just finished praying when the phone
rang and Becky called Linda. "It's for you."

"That's Jack." Her voice was little more than a
hoarse whisper. "I'll have to talk to him—pray for
me."

It was Jack, and he was furious. "What's the big
idea of standing me up? You were supposed to be
down here at seven-thirty. Do you realize I've been
waiting for twenty minutes?"

Linda cleared her throat. "I'm sorry, Jack. I tried to call you at home, but you weren't there."

"I told you that I wanted to meet you down here at seven-thirty and that's what I meant." His voice raised. "Now, get yourself down here! I'm not waitin' for you all night!"

"That's why I called your home," she went on. "I wanted to tell you that I wouldn't be coming to meet you." She was surprised that she was so calm and sure of herself.

"Wh-what did you say?" Jack stammered.

"I called to tell you that I wasn't coming!"

For almost a minute he did not speak. She would have thought he had hung up on her if she had not been able to hear his heavy breathing.

"Listen here, Linda Penner!" he cried. "If you ever want to go with me again you'd better get down here fast. If you stand me up tonight, you and I are through! Understand?"

"That's one of the things I wanted to tell you, Jack," she said. "I'm not going with you anymore."

"What?" He was incredulous.

"I've finally come to see that a Christian shouldn't date a non-Christian. I'm sorry I told you that I would go with you tonight, Jack. I—"

She didn't get to finish what she was saying. His phone slammed in her ear.

Linda smiled her relief. "Well, that's that."

Elsie came over and put an arm about her shoulders. "My dear, I'm so proud of you."

* * *

Across town, Kent was also noting the time. Seven-thirty and he was supposed to be meeting Jack and the guys in half an hour. He went to his bedroom door and watched Danny and Kay with growing impatience. Ordinarily it seemed as though they scurried to get to church early on prayer meeting night, but this night—of all nights—they acted as though they didn't care whether they made it or not. Finally he could stand it no longer. He went in to where they were.

"Danny," he said, "we're going to prayer meeting tonight, aren't we?"

"We always go to prayer meeting." The young missionary pilot looked at his watch. "There's no hurry. We've still got plenty of time."

"But we usually leave a bit earlier than this, don't we?"

"Only if we're picking up someone else." He laid aside his paper. "And we're not doing that tonight."

Before long everyone was ready and they drove away. Jim wanted Kent to sit by him at church but the younger boy shook his head. "Nope. I'm sittin' back here." He chose a place in the corner near the door, a place where he could slip out without being seen.

Midway through the opening song he started to

cough and got to his feet as though he was going outside until he stopped coughing. Once out of the basement room, however, he tiptoed up the stairs and slipped outside.

Checking carefully once more to be sure that he wasn't seen, he stole away. It was only half a dozen or so blocks to the meeting place, but he was late. He scurried up the alley, a block north, and up another alley to the big old barn that was their meeting place. Panting heavily, he joined the group.

They all turned to look at him as he came in. Anger twisted Jack's face and his voice was a snarl. "Where've you been?"

"I told you I'd have trouble gettin' out. I had to wait till Danny and Kay went to prayer meeting, and tonight it took a lot longer'n usual."

Jack stared at him belligerently. "Are you sure it ain't because you're chicken?"

Kent swore to show the others how tough he was. "You know better'n that."

"OK, but don't let it happen again. See?"

Riley spoke up quickly. "Lay off the kid, Jack," he ordered crisply. "We ain't got time for that now."

Jack nodded. Then deliberately he turned his attention to the four younger fellows who were standing together. "Now, this is what we're after tonight." He took a deep breath. "We've got a guy who wants us to get him some tires."

Kent sucked in his breath sharply. Tires! That

was even worse than stealing hubcaps. Fear tightened in iron bands about his thin chest. How could they ever get the tires off a car without getting caught?

6

Kent Runs

Kᴇɴᴛ Gɪʟʙᴇʀᴛ wasn't the only one who was afraid to steal tires. One of the other boys protested quickly.

"How're we goin' to get the tires off a car without someone seein' us?" he asked. "That's what I want to know."

"Me too," somebody else said. "Snitchin' hubcaps is one thing, but tires!" He shivered fearfully.

Jack Ross laughed. "It's not going to be as bad as it sounds."

"What do you mean by that?" Kent demanded.

"We'll tell you all about it on the way to where we're goin'. And we'll also tell you why we had to meet so early tonight."

Each boy was assigned his responsibility. One was to be a lookout in one direction; one in another, and the rest were supposed to do the work. Riley gave the final instructions.

"You'd better start out first, Jack," he said. "Drive slow down Front Street, go over two blocks and back. I'll drive by the warehouse and see if the coast is clear."

"Whew!" Kent gasped. "The warehouse?" he exclaimed. "You aren't figgerin' we can break in there, are you?"

"Pipe down!" Riley snarled. "You talk too much!" Once more he directed his attention to Jack. "If everything's all right I'll blink my lights three times. Then you can drive over there. I'll meet you, and we'll get to work. OK?"

"OK."

Numbly the younger boys got in the car.

When Riley was gone, Kent turned questioningly to Jack. "You ain't figgerin' on us knockin' off no warehouse, are you?"

"You heard what Riley said! Now pipe down!"

Kent shook his head. "Man, if they catch us they'll put us in jail for a million years!"

"They ain't goin' to catch us!" Jack started the car and drove down the alley with his lights off. He did not turn them on until he was almost a block away from the barn. As he drove he gave instructions to the boys.

"I know how you feel about knockin' off this warehouse," he said, hoping his own fear didn't show through. "I don't mind telling you I was a little shook up when Riley first suggested it. Not really scared, mind you. I just didn't see how we could do it without gettin' pinched. Then I got to thinkin' it through, and I began to see how smart old Riley had things worked out. There isn't even a night watchman on duty until almost midnight."

"So that's why we came early," one of the fellows said.

"That's one reason," Jack went on. "Another is that nobody's goin' to expect the warehouse to be knocked off so early in the evening. Guys who pull jobs like this usually wait till the middle of the night. We can slip out there before the night watchman even comes on duty, get the new tires we're after, and be gone in five minutes or so. Nobody'll be the wiser until tomorrow morning when they open up."

All was silent for a moment. Finally one of the boys in the back seat spoke up. "B-but stealin' tires is a lot different than just takin' hubcaps," he stammered. "They'll throw the book at us if we're caught b-b-breakin' into a building."

Jack snorted his derision. "It wouldn't make any difference if we were caught takin' tires out of a building or stealin' hubcaps. Stealin's stealin' and don't you forget it. If a fella gets caught takin' anything, he's had it."

The boy who had been doing the talking was breathing heavily. "Man, I didn't know that. I thought they might let a fella off if he was just caught takin' a little old hubcap."

"The thing we've got to do is to be sure and not get caught," Jack reminded him. "Didn't you hear what Riley said?" he continued. "Smart guys don't get caught—and we're smart."

"But what if we do get nabbed?" the boy persisted uneasily. "What will happen to us? That's what I'd like to know."

"Cut that kind of talk!" Jack growled. "If you're all careful and do as you're told, nobody'll get caught. Nobody at all. Riley and I think as much of *our* necks as you do of yours. You don't think we'd do something like this if we figgered there was a chance of gettin' caught, do you?"

"I—I guess not." But the boy was still far from convinced. That was very apparent.

Kent said nothing, but Jack's boasting did nothing to quiet his own racing pulse. Fear iced his blood and set him to quivering inwardly. Sweat poured down his cheeks although the early spring night was far from warm. His mouth was dry and cottony, and he moistened his lips with his tongue.

If he got through tonight, he'd never go anywhere with Jack again, let alone ever take anything that wasn't his. That was for sure. And he wasn't going to care how much the older boy threatened him either.

Jack continued to talk as he drove. "If my plans

had worked out for tonight, I'd have had me a date to help cover up where I'm going," he said. "Then you guys would've been ridin' with Riley in his car, and I'd be doin' the scouting. But the date didn't work out," he laughed scornfully. "She went religious on me all of a sudden, so here we are."

They met a police car and everyone quit talking suddenly. For a minute or two the occupants of the car were breathlessly quiet. The cops knew, Kent thought inwardly. How could they help but know? At the next corner they would turn around and follow them, and at the warehouse they'd close in and it'd all be over. Fearfully he turned and looked over his shoulder.

Although he thought he did it unobtrusively, Jack saw him.

"What're you lookin' at them for, Kent?" he demanded, his voice jeering. "They don't suspect a thing. They aren't after us. How many times do I have to tell you that?"

"I ain't wantin' them to be after us neither," the boy retorted.

"Forget it. If you keep up that kind of talk you'll get us all jumpy." The driver turned a corner, still following Riley's detailed directions. "You won't be so jumpy when we start divvying up the dough we're goin' to get for tonight's work."

He took a deep breath.

"According to Riley we just got peanuts for those

hubcaps we've been liftin'. Peanuts." He turned again. "It's just like Riley was sayin' yesterday. We've been takin' a lot of risks for almost nothin'. But tonight we're all goin' to get some real work done." He paused significantly. "You guys've been takin' the same risks Riley and I have taken and we appreciate it. We're goin' to treat you right. We figger you've earned a good-sized chunk of the money we get, and you're goin' to get your share."

One of the fellows in the back seat who had said nothing until that moment, piped up quickly. "That sounds great!"

"You stick with us," Jack continued, "and do as we tell you to, and we'll see that you get paid plenty. We take good care of our friends."

On the other occasion when the boys had been nervous about stealing hubcaps Jack had been able to get their minds on the seriousness of the thing they were about to do by talking to them about the money they would soon have. But as far as Kent was concerned, this time it didn't work. He was still as frightened as ever.

At the far end of the street Kent saw a car approaching. His body stiffened and his eyes narrowed. Somehow he knew it was Riley—even before they were close enough for him to really see who it was.

Sure enough—the lights of the other car blinked three times in quick succession.

Somebody in the back seat coughed nervously, and Jack expelled his breath in a thin whistle.

"The coast is clear, fellas," he said, struggling to control his voice. "We're goin' over to the warehouse." Fear broke his voice. "Now, how about it? Do you all know what you're supposed to do?"

They all replied, but with doubtful affirmative.

"Let's go over it once more. Kent, what are you supposed to do?"

Kent swallowed hard. "I—I'm supposed to go into the w-w-warehouse with Riley and—and help him get the tires and load 'em."

"Eddie?"

"I'm the north lookout."

And so it went. Each fellow explained his job. At last Kent asked Jack the question that all four of them had been thinking.

"While we're doin' our jobs, how about you? What're you s'posed to do?"

Jack swore angrily. "That's none of your business! I've got me a job and I'll be doin' it. You don't have to worry about that! You just be sure that you do what you're s'posed to do!"

At the next corner he turned toward the warehouse. Kent leaned back in the seat and closed his eyes. His breath was coming in long, tearing gasps and his heart was racing. He wasn't going to get himself into a mess like this again. That was for sure!

* * *

At prayer meeting the pastor had concluded the short Bible study and was about to lead the group in prayer.

"Are there any prayer requests?" he asked.

Danny was the first to hold up his hand. "I don't know why, Pastor Reeves, but I have a terrific burden for Kent Gilbert this evening. I'd certainly appreciate prayer for him."

* * *

Jack professed to be calm and unconcerned about what they were going to do, but Kent saw that there was a hard set to his jaw and a queer light flickering in his eyes. Sweat beaded the older boy's forehead and his hands were trembling on the steering wheel.

"What's the matter, Jack?" Kent asked. "Are you scared?"

"Scared?" His voice raised angrily. "Me scared? Whatever gave you that idea? Of course I ain't scared!"

He would have said more, but they were so close to the warehouse that there wasn't time. He turned in the direction of the big, dark building and switched off the lights on the car.

One of the boys gasped. "Man, it's dark! D-d-do we have to drive without the lights on?"

"We can't go wheelin' in here with our lights on,

stupid. That's the best way I know to get the cops here on the double!" Just inside the gate he stopped. Riley's car was already there. "All right. Everybody out."

They did as they were told reluctantly.

"And don't forget what you're supposed to do!"

Riley motioned to them. Kent started to creep forward stealthily. He and the older man were going up to the warehouse, find the door in the darkness, and go inside!

He paused for an instant. He couldn't go on! He didn't care what Jack or Riley did to him. He wasn't going to take part in a robbery like this and get caught.

Riley had motioned to him once and moved off into the darkness. For a dozen steps or so Kent followed him hesitantly. Then he saw the big clump of bushes near the path. He moved behind the bushes, veered sharply away from the warehouse, and went running at top speed toward the gate at the far side of the tall wire fence that surrounded the building.

Jack had seen him! He was sure about that! He couldn't have helped it! But he dared not stop now! Neither Jack or Riley was ever going to get him into a mess like this again.

Kent had reached the fence and was climbing over the gate when out of nowhere three police cars came driving into the big gate Riley had left open, their sirens wailing!

7

The Police Arrive!

KENT STOPPED SUDDENLY and turned. For one terrifying moment he stared back at the warehouse. All was confusion. Officers were running about, shouting orders. Powerful searchlights were sweeping the grounds picking up first one terrified figure and then another. All of this Kent watched, transfixed, fear immobilizing his young body.

Breath tore from the boy's aching lungs in great, sobbing draughts. Stark-naked fear gleamed in his eyes, and his slight body shook violently, as though from shock.

The cops had caught Jack and Riley and Eddie and the others! It wouldn't be long until they'd have him too! He had to get out of there!

Whirling, Kent dashed across the deep ditch and into the brush. Branches tore at his clothes and slapped him in the face, but he scarcely noticed. At any moment the police would be heading in his direction. He had to keep moving—moving—moving.

However, it all ended as quickly as it had begun. The confusion and noise at the warehouse subsided. The patrol cars began to pull away. Kent sighed, suddenly weak with relief. But only for a moment! It wasn't over for him yet. It hadn't even started for him!

Jack had probably already squealed on him. That's what he had said he would do if he got caught! He said he'd talk enough to take the whole gang to jail with him!

Maybe the patrol cars were coming over to find him now! Maybe— Lungs screaming for breath, he fought in desperation for more speed. But he could ot move any faster than he was moving already. Exhaustion dragged against his legs with leaden fingers until he almost fell, but he staggered upright and kept running.

He dared not stop! He had to keep going, even faster than before! If he didn't, he would be caught for sure and be thrown in jail. And that would be the end of him. Danny sure wouldn't do anything about getting him out. He'd let him stay in jail until he rotted. That was all Danny cared about him.

At that instant Kent stubbed his toe on a hidden root, stumbled, and fell headlong on the ground. An agonizing sob escaped his lips as he lay there panting. But even falling did not stop him for long. He

scrambled to his feet and stumbled forward. Only
one thought kept hammering through his mind. He
had to get as far from there as possible. He had to
keep driving with all the strength he possessed.

In his fear Kent seemed to think that he could hear
the officers in the brush behind him, and that they
were gaining on him with every stride. From somewhere within his terror-stricken, tortured body he
summoned a new burst of speed. Up a slight hill he
dashed, turned abruptly, and crossed the railroad
tracks. In frantic haste he slid down the rocks and
cinders on the other side of the hill. Once in the park
that bordered the railroad property he dropped,
totally exhausted, behind an outdoor fireplace. He
lay there, motionless, forcing air into his flaming
lungs and trying not to think.

How long he lay there he did not know, but surely
it was no longer than four or five minutes. Slowly the
fire in his lungs went out and he sat up numbly and
looked about. The cops hadn't caught him yet. That
was one good thing. Hope flooded his being momentarily. Maybe he wasn't going to be caught!

Suddenly he realized that the park was lighted.
Not very well, to be sure, but well enough to reveal
his small figure to anyone who happened to be looking for him. A great, icy dread seized him by the
throat. He clambered to his feet and dashed for the
shadows. For the space of a minute or two he stopped
there, grateful for the darkness.

Why did he ever let himself get mixed up with a character like Jack in the first place? he asked himself. Danny and Kay had both tried to warn him. Even Jim had tried to tell him what would happen. Actually he hadn't needed any warning. He knew the kind of a guy Jack was! But he didn't pay any attention to his own good judgment or what anybody else said. He was too smart for that! And now he was going to be caught and put in jail for he didn't know how long. And there wasn't a thing he could do about it!

Or—or was there?

Maybe he could get back to the prayer meeting at church before it was over. If he could, Danny and Kay would vouch for him if anything came up. They'd have to tell the authorities that he was in church all evening. And that would be the end of that. Danny was so honest nobody would ever doubt his word about anything.

For a brief instant, hope surged within Kent's chest again. Maybe he would be able to squirm his way out of this mess without being caught after all.

Cautiously Kent moved along the rim of trees, taking care to stay out of the light as much as possible. He dashed across the street, cut across a lawn, and made his way into an alley.

It was strange, but he had never really liked the dark before. He had never been particularly afraid of it, or anything like that, but he had always preferred the light. Now the darkness was a friend that cloaked his movements and hid him from view.

The church was some distance away, but he managed to reach it. Danny's car was still there, where he had parked it earlier in the evening.

Relief surged through him.

Now if he could just sneak in one of the back entrances, everything would work out for him.

Stealthily he advanced to the back door, opened it, and slipped inside. He could hear the leader of the junior group just bringing the prayer session to a close. He had timed it just right. In a minute all the kids would be filing out of the prayer room and he would be just one of the group. No one would know the difference.

He was smiling his relief. Things had worked out all right after all. Let Jack talk. He had a perfect alibi.

A couple of the fellows about his age came out and he started talking with them.

"I didn't expect to see you here tonight, Kent," one of them said.

For an instant fear leaped to his eyes. "Why not?"

"After that English test Miss Madsen said we're having tomorrow I thought you'd stay home and study."

"That's prob'ly what I should've done, but Danny made me come to prayer meeting."

Jill came up just then. Her gaze fastened on him questioningly.

"Now what're you lookin' at?" he demanded irritably.

"You."

"Me? For cryin' out loud! I thought it was bad enough havin' Danny and Kay watch everything I do. Now they've got you doin' it too."

"You didn't stay for prayer meeting, Kent," she announced.

"I did too!"

"No, you didn't. I saw you go out right after we started singing the first song tonight."

He managed a sickly little laugh.

"Oh, that," he said. "Well, I wasn't feeling very good for awhile. I got to coughing something awful right after the meeting started, so I went out and got some fresh air. But I came right back. I was back before we finished singing the first song."

"I was watching, Kent," she continued. "And I didn't see you."

"Well, I came back just the same."

Jill said nothing more, but Kent had the feeling that she didn't believe him.

In the car Danny asked them what book they had studied that evening. Kent waited for Jill to answer, but she didn't.

Finally she spoke up. "Ask Kent," she said.

said. "As a matter of fact, I've been very discouraged myself the last few weeks. Kent seems so determined to go his own way, and not to have anything to do with the Lord." There was a long silence. "You know, Kay, it's strange, but I had a real burden to pray for Kent tonight. A greater burden than I've ever had before."

Kay nodded. "He has been on my mind in a very special way tonight. I wonder if he's in some kind of trouble."

Danny's mouth firmed, but for the space of a minute or two he said nothing.

"The Lord may have to deal with him very harshly, my dear. We must be prepared for that."

Kay picked at the design in the tablecloth uneasily. "I know you're right. But I can't help hoping that he'll yield before he gets into real trouble."

"If he's not already in real trouble," Danny added.

In his room Kent sat on his bed, staring at the floor. He would never be able to get away with it now. Jack or Riley or one of the other guys would squeal on him. That was for sure. Maybe they'd even think that he had been the one who tipped off the cops. If they thought that, he'd be in real trouble even if the police didn't get him. That Riley was no guy to double-cross!

He got nervously to his feet and walked to the window. It might even be better having the police get him than Riley and Jack! At least he *knew* what the cops would do!

Uncertainly he turned on his heel and started for the other part of the house. Halfway to the door he paused. What should he do? What could he do in a mess like this?

Anger welled within him.

He knew better than to get involved in a deal like stealing hubcaps or anything else. It was his own fault that things had worked out the way they had, and he was in such a terrible jam. There was one thing sure. If he ever got out of this mess, he'd sure never get into another one!

A car drove slowly by the house and stopped. A uniformed police officer stepped out and walked up to the house.

The cops!

They had already caught up with him! He shivered uncontrollably as he heard the doorbell ring!

8

Kent Tells All

K<small>ENT'S</small> <small>FACE</small> <small>BLANCHED.</small> Sweat
gleamed on his forehead and he sucked in his breath
sharply. The police car had stopped!

This was it! The cops knew he had been in on the
warehouse robbery and were coming to get him!
He'd go to jail now for sure! There wasn't any way
out for him! His hand trembled as he ran it across
his face.

For an instant or two he remained motionless, lis-
tening intently.

"Mr. Orlis," the officer was saying. "This is just a
routine check. A couple of boys from the children's
home where Kent and Jill used to live ran off tonight.
We thought possibly they might have come to see
Kent."

"There hasn't been anyone around here," Danny

replied. "But, of course, we just got home. We were at church this evening."

Kent breathed heavily. They hadn't come for him after all. They were just looking for some runaway kids. But that didn't mean they wouldn't still find out. If they didn't learn the truth tonight they would tomorrow. There was only one thing to do. He had to tell Danny the whole story.

Resolutely he moved toward the kitchen.

"Danny!"

The youthful missionary looked up. "Yes?"

"I—I've got to talk to you."

Danny nodded. "Come on in the living room where we can sit down in some comfortable chairs."

Danny moved toward the door but Kent did not follow him. "I—I'd like to talk to you alone."

"Kay's the only one who's up, and I don't keep any secrets from her."

Kent scowled. "I ain't talkin' in front of no woman." He breathed deeply. "If I can't talk to you alone, I ain't talkin'. That's all there is to it."

"We can go in your bedroom, if you like, Kent."

"That's better."

Neither spoke until the door closed behind them.

"Now," Danny said, "what do you want to talk to me about?"

The boy's lips were quivering and his usually defiant eyes filled with tears.

"I—I—" His voice choked and he had to try again. "Danny, I—I'm in a lot of trouble."

"Suppose you sit down and tell me all about it."

Kent scrubbed at his eyes with his knotted fist. "Danny, th-th-there was a r-r-robbery in town to-night."

"I know. We heard about it on the radio after coming home from church." Danny eyed Kent curiously, but did not question him.

"I—I wasn't in on it," the boy stammered falteringly, "but I—I almost was."

Hurt flashed in Danny's eyes. "What do you mean?"

"It was this way," Kent began. Then hesitantly he told Danny everything that had taken place, from the first time Jack Ross picked him up in his car until he ran away from Riley when the man started for the warehouse. "But I didn't go with them and rob the warehouse, Danny. Honestly I didn't. I was running away from there even before the police came."

"I believe you, Kent," Danny answered.

"Th-th-th-they can't put me in jail, can they, Danny?" he pleaded.

The missionary's lips tightened. "I'm sure they'll take everything into consideration, Kent, but the fact remains that you did help steal hubcaps. In the eyes of the law you're as guilty as the other fellows were."

Kent reached out impulsively and grasped Danny

by the arm. "Y-y-you won't let them put me in jail, will you?"

Danny chose his words with care. "I can't make any promises, Kent. But you did do the right thing by coming to me and confessing. I'm sure the judge will be much more lenient with you than he would have been otherwise." Danny got to his feet. "You'd better get your coat, Kent."

Fear widened the boy's eyes. "Wh-wh-where are we going?" he asked, scarcely mouthing the words.

"Down to the police station so you can tell them what you've just told me."

Kent swallowed at the lump in his throat. "Do—do I have to?"

"It's the only way."

"Can't you go a-a-and tell them for me?" he asked.

"I'll go with you," Danny said, "but you'll have to do the talking yourself."

"You can tell them. I—I already told you everything there is to tell."

"I could tell them," Danny said firmly, "but should I? I didn't steal any hubcaps." He opened the door. "Come on, Kent."

"I wish I had never seen that Jack Ross!" the boy blurted. "That's what I wish!"

"That's the way it is so often, Kent," Danny replied, keeping his voice calm. "We are so determined to do exactly as we please in spite of every warning that comes our way. We won't listen to anybody. Then, when real trouble comes because of our own sin and stubborn will, we start to feel sorry for ourselves because we didn't follow the good advice we had."

They drove to the police station in silence. Kent sat very quietly, his hands clenched in his lap. When he saw a car or anyone on the street he scooted lower so he wouldn't be seen. At last Danny broke the silence.

"I don't think your running around with Jack made that much difference, Kent," he said. "I think you would have gotten into trouble anyway."

The younger boy sat up and eyed him questioningly. "What do you mean by that? I thought you were the guy who was always warning me against Jack. You kept telling me that he'd get me into trouble if I kept going places with him. Remember?"

"I did warn you about running with Jack. And I still think he was bad medicine for you—the worst possible thing that could have happened to you. But that doesn't give you an excuse to blame everything that happened on Jack Ross."

"I don't care what you think," the boy went on defensively. "He's the guy who was to blame. He's the one who thought of all the stuff we were doing. He found a place to sell it, and made most of the money too. I don't know why you're trying to blame it all onto me."

"I'm not trying to blame everything on you, Kent," Danny tried to explain. "This is what I'm driving at.

Jack did influence you to do worse things than you would have done on your own, I'll go along with that. But he didn't *make* you steal."

"I don't get what you're driving at," Kent answered.

"You ran around with Jack because you had already made a decision for Satan," Danny said. "You had given your life to the devil and he has been controlling you. Because of that you enjoyed being with Jack." The youthful missionary pulled up to the police station and stopped. "That's why I said you would have gotten into some sort of trouble anyway. Your big problem is not Jack and the way he influences you. Your problem is Satan and the fact that you belong to him."

Kent squirmed uncomfortably. "I can tell you this much. If I get out of this mess, I ain't ever goin' to steal nothin' else as long as I live."

" 'I'm not going to steal anything else,' " Danny corrected him.

"It don't make no difference how you say it, I ain't —I mean, I'm not goin' to take anything that belongs to anyone else—ever."

"I hope you'll always remember that, Kent," Danny told him. "If you do, all this trouble you're going through right now will have accomplished something worthwhile."

They got out of the car and approached the police station. Kent's trembling hand sought Danny's arm.

The two of them went into the police station and the frightened boy blurted out his story to the officer in charge.

He waited patiently until Kent had finished.

"I'm glad you came in, Kent," he said. "We were just going out to get you."

Kent started. "Y-you were?" he stammered. "But how did you know that I had anything to—" His voice choked and trailed away.

A faint smile lifted the corners of the officer's mouth. "Your good friend, Jack Ross, has been telling us everything about everyone in an effort to save his own little neck," he said. "He told us all about your part in this attempted robbery."

"But I didn't have anything to do with stealing those tires from the warehouse," Kent said. "As soon as I got the chance I ran like everything. I was half a block away when the police came."

The officer made no specific comment in reply to Kent's alibi. However, he wrote down everything the boy had told him, then had him read it over and sign that it was true. Once that was accomplished he turned to Danny.

"Do you want him to stay here tonight?"

"I'd like to have him go home with me, if I may," he said. "Are you allowed to accept bail in a case like this?"

The police officer reached for the phone. "I'll call the county attorney and see what he has to say. I think he may be willing to release the boy to you without bail."

He talked with the county attorney for a minute or two while Kent and Danny waited. At last he hung up and turned back to the missionary.

"He said that it would be all right for you to take the boy home with you, Mr. Orlis. All we ask is that you have him back here tomorrow morning at ten o'clock. We would like to talk with him a little more."

"He'll be here," Danny assured him. "And thank you for calling the attorney for me. I appreciate that a great deal."

Dazedly Kent walked ahead of Danny out into the street.

"Wh-wh-what are they going to do to me tomorrow morning?" he asked, his voice small and weak.

"I don't really know," Danny said. "It may be that they just want to question you a little more about what you fellows have done and your part in the whole operation. Or it may be that they will call in a judge and have a trial."

"You—you mean they may have a trial so—so soon?"

Danny nodded.

"Yes, but I think you will find the judge will be very fair."

Fearfully Kent took Danny's arm once more. "Will

they put me in jail, Danny?" he demanded. "Will they?"

"I hope not."

The young missionary's answer startled the frightened boy.

"Why should you care anyway?" he asked curiously. "I should think you'd be glad to get rid of me. I haven't been anything but trouble for you ever since Jill and me came to live with you."

There was a short silence.

"Why didn't you let them keep me down in jail tonight?" Incredulity crept into Kent's voice. "That's what my old man would have done."

"I don't know." Danny spoke frankly. "To be honest with you, Kent, I wondered what would be best for you. But I couldn't stand the thought of your staying down there tonight."

Kent's eyes searched Danny's face thoughtfully. He shook his head as though something he read there wasn't easy to understand.

"I don't get it, Danny," he went on. "I don't get it at all. I've been tellin' Jill that you and Kay don't really care anything about us—that you just want the money the state pays you for taking care of us."

"That isn't it at all," Danny countered. "Both Kay and I love you and Jill a great deal. We're concerned about you. We want to see you grow up into fine, respectable Christians. We want to help you."

The boy shook his head in bewilderment.

"But why?" he asked. "We're nothin' to you."

"That's not true. That's not true at all. You both mean a great deal to us. We love you."

Still Kent could not understand it.

"That's what bugs me. You haven't got no cause to care anything for us."

"Part of the reason we love you is because we have taken the Lord Jesus Christ as our Saviour," Danny said. "Because we're Christians, we want to follow His commandment to love others."

Kent started to speak, but a great lump came up in his throat. Danny stopped the car. As soon as he did so, his young passenger got out and walked toward the house. There was a queer look on his face.

At the back door he stopped and turned, anguish glittering in his eyes. The conversation of a moment or two before was forgotten.

"Danny!" he cried, his voice breaking. "Danny, what are they going to do to me?"

9

Kent in Suspense

Jɪᴍ Mᴏʀɢᴀɴ came down to breakfast a bit earlier than usual the next morning. Kay and Danny were already up and dressed, and breakfast was almost ready.

"Hey," he said, "I heard on the radio just now that they got Jack Ross last night but good!"

Danny nodded. "That's right. They caught him and his friends in the act of robbing a warehouse."

Jim pulled out a chair and sat down at the table.

"Was Kent in on it?" he asked.

Danny hesitated.

"Well," the boy continued, "was he?"

"Not on the warehouse robbery. He had been helping Jack and his gang steal hubcaps and things like that. But on this job he got scared and ran just as the others started for the building. He didn't actually help with it."

"I knew it." A note of triumph crept into Jim's voice. "I knew it! I tried to talk to Kent about Jack. I tried to tell him what kind of a character he was, but Kent wouldn't listen to me. Now I'll bet he wishes he had."

Danny scowled disapprovingly at Jim. "I'm quite sure he does. In fact, I'm sure he's very sorry about a lot of things."

Jim began to butter the toast for Kay as he sat there waiting for breakfast.

"What do you think they'll do to him?"

"I don't know," Danny replied. "I imagine it will depend on how much of his story the judge believes."

"If I was going to be there to testify, he wouldn't believe any of it," Jim retorted self-righteously. "As far as I'm concerned, that Kent is a phony."

Disapproval gleamed in Danny's eyes. "Kent is a boy who needs the Lord Jesus Christ. He's a sinner —a boy who has been deep in sin. But that's all the more reason why he needs to be saved."

Jim frowned. "You sound as though you're sticking up for him."

"I took him to the authorities," Danny went on mildly. "I'm not trying to stick up for him. But I am Kent's friend and I intend to help him in every way I can."

Kent came into the kitchen at that moment, his thin young face twisted with apprehension and fear.

Danny and Kay both spoke to him but he only grunted in return.

Jim smirked. "Hi, Kent. You look as though you stayed up all night. What's the matter, couldn't you sleep?"

Anger flickered in Kay's eyes and her voice raised. "Jim Morgan!"

He grinned again indulgently and looked away. Kent's pale young face colored a livid red and his eyes carried a gray, haunted look. He eyed Jim first, and then Danny. At last he turned and started for the other room.

"Breakfast will be ready in just a minute, Kent," Kay told him.

"I ain't hungry."

Danny started to correct him, but checked himself.

The door closed behind Kent. Kay watched as he disappeared from view, concern darkening her kind eyes.

"Poor Kent," she said. "I don't think I've ever seen anyone as miserable as he is right now."

Jim drew himself up haughtily. "He ought to be miserable. He just ought to be, after all the things he's done."

Danny frowned his disapproval. "Jim, that's not a very good Christian attitude toward someone who's in trouble."

"I haven't seen anything very Christian about

Kent," he retorted. "When I see him start to live like a Christian, I'll start treating him like one."

Danny would have answered him, but Kent opened the kitchen door. "Danny," he said, "do I have to go to school be-before I—I—before ten o'clock?"

Danny shook his head. "No, I think it would be just as well for you to stay here."

Jim got up and went into the other room.

"I think I'll go get my books while you're finishing breakfast, Kay," he said. "I'd better get to school a little early this morning."

Kay tried to get Kent to come in and eat, but he stayed in his room until after Jim was gone. Even though he did come to the table then, he only sat there and toyed with the food on his plate.

"Jim hopes that I'll go to jail," he said at last.

Kay came over and sat down beside him.

"Oh, no, he doesn't," she countered. "Jim knows that Christ is the answer to all your problems, and he wants to see you become a Christian. That's all."

But Kent was not dissuaded. "That's not the way he feels about me at all," he said. "He wants them to put me in jail. I can tell by looking at him."

Kay did not answer him directly.

"Kent," she said, "don't you think you ought to let the Lord take control of your life?"

His gaze met hers momentarily, then he turned away. "I'm goin' to be different from now on," he told her. "When I get out of this mess, I'm never goin' to get into no more trouble. And that's for sure."

"I hope that's right, Kent," she said, "but the Bible tells us that we are all sinners. So, we sin and keep right on sinning. We can decide that we're not going to do something, but the chances are we won't be strong enough to keep from it unless we have the Lord Jesus Christ to help us."

"I'm goin' to start goin' to church and stuff like that, better'n I used to."

"Going to church is fine, Kent. But that isn't enough. We have to recognize that we are sinners, lost and in need of a Saviour. And we have to be concerned enough to do something about it. If we don't all the going to church in the world won't help us any."

He pushed back from the table. "They'll prob'ly put me in jail where I won't have no chance to go to church," he blurted, "even if I wanted to." With that he shuffled dejectedly into the other room.

At last the time arrived for him and Danny to go down to the courthouse. At first they had decided that just Danny and Kent would go. However, at the last minute Kay decided to go along.

Kent protested belligerently. "There's nothin' you can do down there," he said. "I don't see why you've got to be there."

"I wouldn't feel right if I didn't go," she said simply.

"Why not?" Questions gleamed in his eyes. "What's it to you?"

"I love you." She put a hand on his shoulder tenderly but he shook it off.

"OK. If you've got to go I guess it'll have to be all right with me. But I sure don't see why you've got to be bothered."

They went down to the courthouse where the other boys and their parents had gathered. Jack was sitting on the front seat, his mother and father on either side of him. He glared at Kent when he came in.

Each of them was being tried separately and there were several attorneys present to plead the cases of Riley, Jack, and at least two of the other boys. However, that did not make it any easier for them.

"Two to five years in the State Penitentiary at Stillwater," the judge announced in deciding Riley's case.

Kent swallowed hard and tears came to his eyes. It was going to be his turn before long. He wouldn't get off any easier than Riley did. That was for sure.

Jack was next. He came before the bench and looked down at the floor as the judge gave him his sentence. "One to three years in the Reformatory at St. Cloud."

Then the court turned its attention to the younger boys who had been involved. Each told his story and was questioned by the judge. By this time they didn't look like the swaggering, cigarette-smoking bunch of guys Kent had been running with. Tears coursed down their cheeks, and one sobbed openly.

Kent was the last to be heard. He told the judge about his part in helping to steal hubcaps, and how he had run from the warehouse before Jack and Riley and the others broke open the lock on the big door.

"You're a ward of the state, aren't you, Kent?" the judge asked when he had finished.

Kent eyed him questioningly. "What does that mean?"

"Didn't the County Welfare Office place you with the Orlis family?"

"Oh, yeah. I—I guess so."

The judge riffled through the papers on his desk. "I'm going to continue your case for one week so the Welfare Office can have an opportunity to make recommendations."

Kent swallowed hard, and for an instant or two it looked as though he was going to ask the judge a question, but he did not.

The judge turned to Danny. "Mr. Orlis, I'm placing Kent Gilbert in your custody," he said gravely. "We will hear his case a week from today at ten o'clock."

Mechanically Kent left the stand and walked out to the car with Danny and Kay. Fear glittered in his eyes, and when he spoke, his voice quavered.

"Wh-wh-what do you think they're going to do to me, Danny?" he asked.

Danny shook his head. "We'll just have to wait a week and see."

"Why do you s'pose they want the Welfare Office checkin' into it?" he persisted.

"You're a ward of the state, Kent," Danny explained. "The Welfare Office has to be considered. That's their responsibility."

The boy's lips curled disgustedly. "I don't know why. They ain't never done nothin' for me."

They reached the car and got in.

"I'm sure the Welfare Office has done more for you than you give them credit for doing," Danny said.

Kent slumped into the seat, his face growing even more taut than before.

"I don't see why that judge couldn't have decided today what to do with me," he said. "I don't see why I've got to wait a whole week."

* * *

Jim learned the outcome of the trial that afternoon from some of the kids at school.

"Hey, Jim," one of the fellows said, hurrying to catch up with him. "What was the matter with that judge anyway? He left all those guys, except Riley and Jack, get off scot-free."

"Not exactly. The guys weren't sent to jail, but they're on probation. They've really got to watch what they do or they'll be in a worse mess," Jim replied.

The other boy sneered.

"They're on probation," he echoed. "What does that amount to?"

Jim opened his locker and took out some books. "I've got to admit I agree with you. I don't think they should've been so easy on them. I think that judge ought to've made an example out of them so other kids would know what will happen if they get into that kind of trouble."

"Yeah," his companion agreed. "And that Kent who lives at your house. I hope they give it to him but good!"

When Jim got home from school he told Kay what the kids at school had been saying.

"And they're right too," he concluded. "You ought to let the Welfare Office have Kent and Jill back." His voice rose indignantly. "That's what you ought to do! They don't deserve a home like this!"

10

Jim Rubs It In

KAY RAISED HER VOICE. "Jim!" she exclaimed. "You don't mean that! You can't!"

"I never meant anything more in my whole life," he retorted. "They ought to take that Kent Gilbert and stick him in a reformatory the way they did Jack Ross. He doesn't deserve to live in a home like you and Danny have given him."

For the space of a minute Kay stared at Jim with a bewildered and hurt look in her soft brown eyes. When she spoke she was more sorrowful than angry, and she looked as though she was about to cry.

"Jim," she said, "I didn't think we would ever hear you make a statement like that. You're a Christian!"

He faced up to her, defiance steeling his young face.

"Kay, that Kent is bad medicine anyway you want to look at it. He's been nothin' but trouble ever since he came to live with us, and he always will be. Everybody seems to know it but you and Danny."

"But Christ could change Kent's life, Jim," she told him. "He could make him a new creature, the same as He has done with you and me. Kent isn't hopeless by any means."

"Maybe not." Doubt edged his voice. "But he's sure gettin' close to it. The more anyone talks with him about the Lord, the more he hardens his heart. He's not about to become a Christian, and there's no use tryin' to work with him. It's just a waste of time."

Kay took a long while in answering.

"Jim," she said, "I don't even like to mention the past. I don't want to hurt you, and I don't want you to think that we're holding it against you, but things weren't too good with you when you first came to live with Mother and Dad Orlis. Do you remember?"

A strange, hurt look came to his eyes.

"I never stole any hubcaps," he said defensively.

"No, it wasn't hubcaps," she continued. "As I recall, you were involved with a fellow stealing fish, and later you helped him to smuggle dope into the country from Canada."

"I—I—" Jim licked his lips nervously.

"If it hadn't been for Mother and Dad Orlis and the way they stood up for you, you would have been put in the reformatory yourself. As I remember, we were all praying for you."

"I—I just got in with the wrong fellow."

"That's right. You got in with the wrong fellow just as Kent did," she said, "and keeping company with the wrong person did the same thing to both of you."

Jim was silent. Anger smoldered in his eyes.

"If Mother and Dad Orlis and Danny and Ron had written you off the way you want to write Kent off, where do you think you would be right now? Do you think you would be a Christian boy and living with us?"

"But it isn't the same," he said defensively. "Kent is just not interested in anything spiritual. He won't even let a fellow talk to him about Christ."

"That's exactly the way you were, Jim," she said, leaning forward. "I suppose we could have decided that we couldn't do anything with you and quit trying. But we all kept bringing you before God in prayer, and He honored our prayers. Finally He brought you to the place where you were willing and ready to accept Him as your Saviour."

Jim swallowed hard. "I still don't think I was as bad as he is."

"It seems to me that you were just as bad as Kent has ever been," Kay persisted. "I know you caused us all a lot of heartache. But that really doesn't make any difference. Actually, there's no degree of sin as far as God is concerned. I'm sure He doesn't see any difference in the way you used to be and the way Kent is now. Or, any difference between either of you and the way I was before I confessed my sin and accepted Him as my Saviour. And I never stole a thing in my life."

Jim ran his hand over his forehead uncertainly.

"You sure make a guy feel cheap," he said.

She smiled to take some of the sting from her words.

"I don't mean to make you feel cheap, Jim," she continued. "I just wanted to remind you of something that's very easy for any of us to forget. So often, when we look at other people, we are a little too quick to criticize them, or to decide that there's no chance of ever winning them for Christ. We ought to remember what our own lives used to be before we made a decision for Him, and pray a little harder for the unsaved person we've been criticizing."

Jim took a deep breath.

"I know what you mean," he said at last. "And I know that you're right. But when I think of the way Kent has hurt you and Danny I get so mad I could explode. He ought to be punished for all the things he's done so he'll know better than to do them again. If he gets off easy this time, he'll do the same thing again as soon as he thinks he can get away with it."

Kay shook her head.

"Kent isn't going to get off completely free, Jim.

I can assure you of that right now. We're not trying to get him out of anything, except to avoid sending him to the reformatory if at all possible."

Jim's voice rose. "But why?" he demanded. "Kent broke the law, didn't he? The way I look at it, he ought to pay the price."

"He'll pay the price for what he's done," Kay countered. "I'm sure that Judge Kelso will see to that. But my chief concern is to see him won for the Lord. Christ is the only foundation on which Kent, or anyone else, can build a new responsible life. That's what Danny and I are working toward. Not to see how easy we can make things for him."

Jim did not answer her.

"Please pray for Kent, Jim," she said. "Pray that he'll take Christ as his Saviour."

"Well, sure. I'll be praying for him. I've been praying for him all the time. I want to see him accept Christ and live the way he should as much as anyone else does." He spoke slowly. "But I still think he ought to pay for all the things he's done."

Kay did not press the conversation further.

*   *   *

That evening Linda went home directly after school. Elsie was sitting in the living room alone, knitting on a sweater.

"Hello, Linda," she said pleasantly. "I didn't expect you to be home so soon."

"I should have gone to the library." The girl

crossed the room and sat down. "But I didn't feel like it tonight."

Elsie's gaze met hers. "You act as though something's bothering you. Is everything all right?"

"I—I guess so." She tied a knot in one corner of her head scarf. Her face was pale and drawn, and her lips were trembling. "As far as I'm concerned everything's all right."

The older woman put aside her knitting. For the space of a minute or so neither spoke.

Finally Linda looked up. "You heard about Jack, didn't you?"

Elsie nodded.

"They told about him over the news a few minutes ago," she said. "He was given one to three years in the reformatory, and Riley got two to five years in the penitentiary."

Tears slipped unheeded from under Linda's long eyelashes.

"I—I can't help but feel badly about it, Elsie," she said. "I—I feel terrible to think that he's not going to get to graduate, but has to go to the reformatory instead. It could ruin his whole life."

The older woman nodded understandingly.

"It's not that I'm in love with him, or anything like that," Linda continued. "You know that I had already given up going with him. But in spite of all the bad things he has done, he's got a lot of good qualities. I can truthfully say that I enjoyed being with him."

"I'm sure you did. I think that's one of the dangers a Christian girl faces when she dates an unsaved fellow. She is apt to find that she really enjoys his company."

"If only he would have confessed his sin and put his trust in the Lord Jesus Christ," Linda said wistfully. "None of this would have happened."

"That would have made all the difference in the world," Elsie agreed.

Linda wiped her eyes and swallowed hard.

"I used to think I could lead him to Christ," she said, her gaze searching the older woman's face. "I tried as hard as I could, but it didn't seem to make any impression on him. He wouldn't listen to me."

Elsie went over and sat down beside her. "You did your part when you witnessed to him," she said as gently as possible. "That was your responsibility. But Jack had to decide what he wanted to do with his life, and he didn't decide for Christ."

Linda sat up very straight. It was a moment or two before she could speak.

"Th-th-there's something else that's been bothering me today," she said, "almost as much as what happened to Jack."

Elsie put an arm about her shoulders.

"Would you like to tell me about it?" she asked.

There was a brief hesitation.

"I don't mean to pry, Linda. And if you'd rather not say anything about it, that will be all right with me."

"It's not that at all." Desperately the girl was fighting against tears. "I want to talk to you, only I—I don't know if I can."

The older woman waited patiently until Linda had control of herself once more.

"I've been thinking how I've been acting off and on for the past year—ever since I've been a Christian. I haven't been living the sort of a Christian life that Robin Evans and some of the other kids live." As she continued her voice firmed. "I get all excited about serving the Lord one minute, and the next I have trouble keeping from going off into the world with the kids who have never even heard of Christ."

"I know just how you feel, Linda," Elsie replied. "Satan attacks each of us where we are the weakest, and you seem to be attracted by worldliness and the good times you think the kids in the world are having."

Linda's eyes widened. "How did you know that?"

"It's right, isn't it?" Elsie continued.

"Yes, I—I guess so. But I didn't really face up to it until today. I didn't think anyone else knew about it."

Elsie smiled winsomely. "Your father and I have been praying about that ever since you became a Christian."

"And I thought I had fooled everybody the way I had been fooling myself." She breathed deeply. "And, Elsie, my love for the things of the world brought me so close to getting into terrible trouble."

"You mean because of Jack?"

"That's right. Do you realize I had made a date with him for the night of the robbery?" she asked. "And I came so close to going with him I get goose bumps just thinking about it. If I had gone with him as I had planned, I—I would probably have been in the car with him when he drove up to the warehouse and the police arrested him. Oh, Elsie, I came so close to making a terrible mess of my life."

"We can thank God that you didn't."

Still Linda was not satisfied. "What I'm afraid of is that it's going to happen again. Maybe God won't be so—so easy with me the next time. Maybe He will let me get into terrible trouble."

"There's one way to be sure that won't happen," her stepmother suggested quietly.

"How's that?"

"You can consecrate your life completely to Christ. If you do, and stay in the center of His will, you won't have anything to be concerned about."

"Will you pray with me?" Linda's voice broke tearfully.

Together Linda and Elsie knelt in the living room and the girl cried out to God. Never in her life had she prayed the way she prayed that day. When at last she finished, Elsie thanked the Lord for hearing and answering their prayers for Linda's life.

When they got to their feet, Linda was smiling radiantly through her tears.

"I feel as though I got out from under a huge load," she said.

"That is actually what happens when we give Christ control of our lives," Elsie continued. "When He takes over, He looks after us and cares for us, and we don't have to carry our burdens ourselves."

"Daddy used to tell me that," Linda said, "but I didn't know what he meant. I've never known what he was talking about until today."

"This is one of the most important lessons we have to learn."

"I'm so glad I learned it before it was too late." Linda sighed deeply. "I don't know why I kept fighting against giving my life completely to Christ. I should have known that He would do a better job of running things than I ever could."

The older woman chose her words with great care.

"You've just made a big step forward in your Christian life, Linda," she said. "It's a very important step. But don't make the mistake of assuming that this is the end as far as Satan's temptations are concerned. Don't think that you can sit back now, secure in the belief that everything will be easy for you from this time on."

The girl stared at her quizzically. "What do you mean?"

"Sometimes when we make a decision like this we simply allow ourselves to become better targets for Satan's arrows. There's a danger in thinking we are really pretty good once we've made a decision of consecration. If we do that, we can be sure that Satan will hit us hard, and in just the weakest place so he'll have the best chance of making us stumble and fall."

Linda's face clouded.

"How can I keep that from happening?" she asked seriously. Her lips trembled as though she was once more on the verge of crying. "I don't *ever* want to get to the place where I'm in danger of drifting away from God again."

"The first thing is to be aware of the fact that it can happen to you, just as I must constantly be aware of the fact that it can happen to me. If we recognize the fact that we are capable of sinning and sinning grievously, we can take steps to prevent it."

"But how?"

"We've got to realize that being a Christian isn't just something that affects us for a little while on Sundays. It's a twenty-four-hour-a-day job, seven days a week, fifty-two weeks a year. And, moreover, we can't withhold any part of our lives for ourselves. We've got to take Christ into every area, regardless of how large or how small."

Linda started to question her, but checked herself as her stepmother continued.

"Then we've got to realize how important it is to have our private devotions each morning. We should read our Bibles and meditate on what we've read; then have a time of prayer each day, as regularly as we brush our teeth."

"I think that's one place where I've fallen down," Linda acknowledged. "I've been trying to have devotions every morning, but it seems as though something always comes up after two or three mornings to keep me from it. Then, the first thing I know, I'm out of the habit."

"Now there is something Satan tries on almost every Christian. He fights daily devotions with everything he can, because he knows that's what strengthens us and helps us to resist temptations."

Linda's mouth firmed. "I had no idea it was so important."

"Private devotions are so important," her stepmother said, "that Christians who have walked with the Lord for years wouldn't think of starting the day without a time of Bible reading and prayer."

Linda breathed deeply.

"And to think," she murmured, "that I tried to live my life as a Christian should without any regular time of devotions."

"Of course, Bible reading and prayer aren't the only things that we must have to keep us true to

Him," Elsie went on. "We must go to church, Sunday school, and prayer meeting regularly each week, and to as many other services as we can manage. We need to fellowship with other Christians, and church is the best place to do it."

"Hmm. I'd never quite thought of church in that way," she said. "I always thought that going to church was something we did for God."

"No, church is for our benefit and help, not just so we can please God by attending."

They continued to talk until Mr. Penner came home for dinner shortly after six o'clock. When they finished there was a bond between the two of them that had not been present before.

11

Danny Intercedes

At the Orlis home, Kent sat nervously at Danny's big desk. His books were piled high before him, but he was scarcely aware of them. He read a paragraph in his history assignment for the fourth time, ran a trembling hand across his forehead, and read the same paragraph once more, without even knowing what it said.

The front door opened and he looked up warily to see who was there.

"Hello, Jim," he said hesitantly, as though he was not entirely sure whether the Morgan boy would speak to him or not.

"Hi." Jim stopped in the middle of the floor. "Where is everybody?"

"Danny and Kay aren't home yet."

Jim stood there momentarily. He seemed to be debating whether to say more or not. Then he crossed to the divan and sat down. Kent watched him apprehensively.

"I heard what happened to you guys," Jim began at last, his voice cold and expressionless. "You were mighty lucky. That's all I can say."

Kent swallowed against the lump in his throat.

"The other guys know what's going to happen to them," he said, "but I don't. I've got to wait a whole week to find out."

Jim shrugged his shoulders. "They won't do any worse to you than they did to anyone else."

"They might." The ice in the pit of Kent's stomach continued to grow. "The Welfare Office has to decide whether I—I have to go to that children's home or not. I might not get to stay with Danny and Kay and you anymore." His voice broke, as though he was close to tears.

Jim saw it, but snorted his disgust.

"I hope you do have to go there," he retorted. "I just hope you do. All you've ever done around here is cause trouble for Danny and Kay and the rest of us since you came here to live."

Kent winced. The color drained from his cheeks. He took a deep breath and sighed.

"I ain't goin' to cause them no more trouble. That's for sure! If I get out of this mess, I won't be gettin' into nothin' else."

A sneer twisted Jim's face. "That's what you say now, but just you wait. If they don't send you to that children's home, you'll be right back where you were before, just as soon as you think you can get away with it."

Kent started to protest, but footsteps sounded on the front step and he turned back to his books.

Jim lowered his voice to a hoarse whisper. "I hope they do send you to the children's home. I hope they do!"

At that moment Kay came into the house, her arms loaded with groceries. When Jim saw her he got up and went quickly to help her.

"Here," he said, "let me take some of those."

He took the groceries and went into the kitchen with her. Once they were alone Kay faced him, her eyes searching his.

"Jim," she said guardedly, "what's wrong?"

"Nothing."

"Were you and Kent arguing when I came in?"

He shook his head.

"We weren't arguing," he said. "I just told him a few things he needed to hear."

Kay waited until the clock finished striking.

"I hope you were kind, Jim," she told him.

"Kind?" The word exploded from his lips. "That joker doesn't need anyone to be kind to him. He needs to have someone tell him where to get off!"

"I thought we had gone over all this, Jim," she replied. "And that you understood."

"I understand, all right." He stormed out the door.

"And if you think I'm going to pat him on the head and tell him to be a good little boy, you've got to guess again. What that guy needs is a good kick in the pants."

Kay watched him walk out of sight. Sorrowfully she turned back to her work in the kitchen. Poor Jim. He was so hard—so unforgiving. As she started the evening meal she prayed for him silently.

*   *   *

Although it seemed as though the day for Kent's trial would never come, it finally did. The night before he was to appear before Judge Kelso he scarcely slept at all. Every time he closed his eyes he could see the stern face of the judge peering down at him from the black robes. Then that vision would fade and he would see the children's home, with the workers he found so distasteful, and the other kids who were as unhappy and miserable as he had been.

He had always done a lot of talking about having to stay with Danny and Kay. He had complained about the discipline, the things they made him eat, and the chores they insisted he do around the house. But staying there was a breeze compared with the home.

And now he was going to have to go back! Scalding tears filled his eyes and trickled down his cheeks. He scrubbed at them angrily with the back of his fists.

What had been the matter with him, anyway?

Why hadn't he listened to all the warnings he'd been given to stay away from Jack? Now he'd have to go back to the children's home and consider himself lucky he hadn't been sent to a worse place, when he could have stayed with Danny and Kay.

Hesitantly he swung his feet over the side of the bed and sat up. He'd run away. That's what he'd do! He wouldn't stick around here and let them put him back in the home! That was for sure!

Kent picked up his trousers and started to get into them when he stopped suddenly.

Running away would only make matters worse. The cops would come after him the way they had come after those two kids who had run away the night of the warehouse robbery. They'd get him before he got two miles out of town! Numbly he crawled back into bed.

There was nothing else to do! He had to stay there and face whatever came! After a time he tried to pray the way he had heard Jim and Danny and Kay pray so many times. But he could not. He didn't even know how to pray!

The next morning he dressed mechanically and waited for the time to go down to the courthouse with Danny and Kay. A Miss Sarah Jennings, whom neither Danny nor Kay had ever seen before, was there to represent the Welfare Office. The judge called on her after the charge against Kent had been read and he pleaded guilty.

"As a case worker for the Welfare Office," Miss Jennings began, "I have made a thorough investigation and find that Mr. and Mrs. Orlis have done everything possible to provide a good home for Kent Gilbert, and to help him to attain respectability and to prepare himself to take an honorable position in our community."

There was a short pause.

"But the boy has strenuously resisted every effort that has been put forward to help him. He has lied to them repeatedly, has been truant from school, and has willfully and deliberately refused to take advantage of any of the opportunities offered to him."

As she finished her description of the way he had rebelled against Danny and Kay's authority, Kent's face blanched.

"And what is your recommendation?" the judge asked her.

"I can see no further point in asking Mr. and Mrs. Orlis to assume the responsibility of the care and discipline of a boy like Kent Gilbert," she said. "He is incorrigible and, in my opinion, any effort that is spent to attempt to restore him to a responsible place in society will be wasted."

A deep hush settled over the courtroom. Kent choked and stared down at the floor.

"Then you think it would be best to send him back to the children's home or to some other institution where they are better equipped to discipline a difficult youngster. Is that right?"

"Exactly."

Danny got to his feet.

"Your Honor," he broke in, "may I say a word?"

The judge leaned forward, clasping his hands together. "Certainly, Mr. Orlis. I was just about to ask you if you would like to comment."

"I didn't come here with the intention of saying anything one way or the other in the trial, but now I have to speak out."

Every eye in the courtroom was fastened on Danny.

"Everything Miss Jennings has said about Kent is true," he began. "He has lied and stolen and cheated. He's arrogant and overbearing, and completely undependable. Humanly speaking, we would have given up on him long ago and would have asked the Welfare Office to take him back."

The judge nodded. "I can well understand why you would feel that way. It makes my decision much easier."

"But, Your Honor," Danny broke in hurriedly, "my wife and I didn't vounteer to take children into our home because we thought it would be easy, or even because it would be a means of making money. We did it because we thought it would provide an opportunity to help children like Kent who so desperately need help."

The judge's forehead crinkled. "I'm not sure that I follow you, Mr. Orlis. Am I to take it that you are asking us to leave the boy in your home, after all that has happened?"

"Yes, Your Honor. We feel that we have an opportunity to work with him—a better opportunity than anyone else—because he has indicated that he still wants to stay with us."

"And you think you can do something with him?" the judge asked incredulously, "after all you've told me about the boy?"

Danny nodded. "With God's help, I think something can be done for him. And with your permission, we would like to try."

The judge pursed his lips thoughtfully.

"I wouldn't say that I am convinced you can do anything with Kent Gilbert," he began at last. "In fact, it would seem to me that you have about exhausted every means at your disposal of reaching him. But I don't see how I can deny a request like that." He turned to Kent and called the boy up to Danny's side. "Young man, have you heard what Mr. Orlis has said about you just now?"

"Y-y-yes, sir."

"You know that both Miss Jennings and I feel that Mr. and Mrs. Orlis would be justified in letting you go back to the children's home, don't you?"

"I—I—I know that."

"I hope you realize what they are trying to do for

you, Kent." His voice was stern. "It is because they still want to work with you that I am considering their request."

Kent's lips were trembling and he brushed nervously at his forehead.

"Because of the Orlises," Judge Kelso concluded, "I am going to allow you to remain in their home on probation. I hope that you justify the faith and trust they are putting in you, and that you don't let them down."

Kent looked at Danny briefly, then he dropped his head and began to sob uncontrollably. Kay went over and put an arm about his shoulders.

"There now, Kent," she said. "Don't cry. Everything's going to be all right."

For the space of a minute or two he could not speak. At last he got control of himself enough to lift his head.

"You're not going to be sorry about this, Kay," he said shakily. "I promise! I'm never goin' to let you down again!"

12

Danny and Kay's Prayer

K<small>ENT COULD HAVE GONE</small> to school
the rest of the day but he objected tearfully to going
back so soon.

"All the kids know about the trial, Danny," he
said hesitantly. "Just as soon as I get back to school
they'll start comin' up to me and tryin' to find out
what happened. W-w-wouldn't it be all right if—if
I wait and go to school tomorrow morning, Danny?"
His voice quavered pathetically.

Danny's tone was kind, but he was not overly
sympathetic.

"I can imagine that it is going to be tough for you
to go back to school and face the kids, Kent," he
said, "but it's not going to be any easier tomorrow.
If you go today, you'll have it over with."

"It wouldn't be over with." He wiped at his eyes
again. "You don't know that bunch out at school.

119

They'll keep after me and after me and after me."
He bit his lower lip. "I just can't go to school this
afternoon."

Danny drove for a block or so without speaking.

"It'll be a lot easier goin' to school tomorrow, Danny," Kent continued. "The kids will all know how
the trial came out and won't be askin' me about it.
They might razz me about everything that's happened, but I—I—" he could not find the words to
continue.

"I know it's going to be hard for you to go back to
school the first few times, Kent," Danny repeated.
"I've seen kids who've had problems with the authorities come back and try to take up where they
left off. It's not easy. But we can't run away from
our problems and troubles. The best thing—in fact,
the only thing—is to face up to them."

"I know that, Danny," Kent answered, "but you
don't know wh-wh-what it's going to be like to have
to go there and face all the kids and know th-th-that
they won't have anything to do with me."

"This is part of the cost of breaking the law," the
young missionary said.

Kent laid his hand on Danny's. "Won't you let me
stay home this afternoon? Please?"

Danny nodded reluctantly.

"Yes, I'll let you stay home this afternoon, Kent.
But that's the only time you'll get to stay home."
The tone in Danny's voice changed. "I don't want to

preach to you right now, fella, but I can't help point-
ing out that this is always the way sin ends. We go
our own way, sinning against God, and sometimes
against the law of our land. We think we're getting
away with it, but all the while we're going deeper
and deeper into sin. Then the time comes when we
have to pay the price for our sin, and we are ab-
solutely miserable."

The boy swallowed hard.

"Boy, you can say that again," he admitted. "I've
learned my lesson, believe me. I'll never steal anything, or do anything to get into trouble ever again.
I've had it! And that's for sure."

"I'm glad to hear you say that, Kent," Danny told
him. "I hope and pray that you stay by it. Practi-
cally speaking, however, there's only one way you
can be sure that you're not going to get into trouble
again."

Warily Kent eyed him.

"And how's that?" he asked.

"By turning your life completely over to the Lord
and letting Him lead and guide you in the way He
wants you to go," Danny said.

"I know a lot of people who haven't done that and
they still don't get into trouble," Kent answered.

"That may be," the young pilot answered, "but
they haven't had the start toward trouble that you've
had, Kent. If you'll think for a minute you'll realize
that you've been in and out of trouble with the

school authorities, the Welfare Office, and the police for the past four or five years. And, as I see it, the pattern's going to continue until you give your life completely to God."

The boy straightened with new determination.

"We'll see about that." As far as he was concerned that ended the conversation.

*   *   *

The next morning Kent dressed for school with considerable reluctance. Danny had to call him several times to get him to hurry.

"If you don't hurry, Kent, you're going to be late."

Kent came dragging into the living room, carrying his shoes and socks in his hand.

"I—I don't feel so good this morning, Danny," he said. "I've got a terrible headache."

"Oh?"

"I—I don't think I feel good enough to go to school today."

"I think you do," Danny answered.

"I didn't sleep at all last night." He yawned. "I'm bushed."

"You'll feel better after you get to school," Danny told him.

After breakfast Kent started slowly for the door. But with his hand on the knob he turned back uneasily.

"I can't go, Danny!" Desperation edged his voice. "I thought I could face the kids this morning, but I can't do it! I'm not goin' out there and have 'em laughin' at me!"

"They won't be laughing at you," the young missionary said. "And it won't make any difference if they do. You have to face them. There's no other choice."

"I could run away." He threw that out speculatively, watching for the reaction.

"If you do you'll not go to the children's home when they catch you," Danny reminded him. "They'll send you to a boy's training school or reformatory."

"Just let me stay home until noon, Danny," he said. "I could face the kids after dinner. I promise."

"You stayed home yesterday afternoon, Kent. You are not staying home today. That's final."

Kent saw that nothing good could come from arguing with Danny, so he got his coat.

"How about taking me to school this morning?" he asked hopefully. "It wouldn't be so bad if I didn't have to walk to school with the kids."

"I'm sorry, Kent, but I've got to go directly to the airport." Danny glanced at his watch. "Besides, you've got plenty of time to walk."

The boy's lips parted to retort angrily, but he checked himself and remained silent.

Kent left the house and made his way slowly down the treelined sidewalk to the junior high school building. Other fellows were going to school that morning too. They were walking in twos or threes, laughing and talking gaily. As he approached, however, they looked his way and their conversation ceased. He didn't want to speak to them, but he had to. Suddenly he realized that he had to have friends. Anybody had to have friends!

"Hi." He spoke with something akin to desperation in his voice.

"Hi." Their replies were taut and hostile.

Kent's cheeks flushed hot. The guys wouldn't have anything to do with him! He'd never have any friends again!

At the next street corner Kent hesitated. He couldn't go on to school and be treated that way by the kids. He couldn't have them staring at him as though he were a criminal or something. He'd play hooky. That's what he'd do. He'd show Danny that he didn't have to jump every time he said something!

Kent took half a dozen steps up a side street before pausing once more. It'd serve 'em right if he played hooky, but if he did Danny would call the judge and the stupid old character would throw the book at him. He'd wind up in jail for sure! No, he had to go on to school. No matter how hard it would be to go, he couldn't play hooky again.

Each step toward the big, forbidding brick building was agony, but he had to go on. He savagely kicked a stone with his toe, as though it had been the cause of all his troubles. What had been the matter with him in the first place?

Again he asked himself about Jack. Why had he gotten mixed up with a guy like that anyway? He'd been warned about running with Jack often enough and by enough different people. If he'd been halfway smart he'd have followed their advice.

It was his own fault that he had gotten himself into the mess he was in. He was a big dope! That was all there was to it! It served him right to be in trouble!

Kent never did know how he got through the day. Nobody spoke to him unless they had to, and when he met his former friends in the corridors they seemed to shrink away from him as though they were ashamed that they had ever known him. And they were the guys who had thought he was hot stuff when he was running around with Jack. They were the guys who talked to him about playing hooky with them, and things like that.

When classes were finally out for the day, the boy left the building as hurriedly as possible and went directly home.

Kay was in the living room when he entered. She looked up, smiling.

"Hello, Kent."

He did not answer her.

"How'd school go today?"

"Terrible."

"That's too bad. I don't know whether or not it helps any, but I'm sure that it will wear off before long. In a couple of weeks they'll all be treating you as though nothing ever happened."

"I can't do it, Kay." He spoke with finality. "I just can't face 'em again! And what's more, I ain't goin' to!"

"You aren't going to," she corrected.

"That's what I said. I ain't goin' to."

"I was correcting your English, Kent," she reminded him gently. "I wasn't agreeing with what you were saying."

"Kay, you don't know how hard it is for me to have to go to school and not have any of the kids even speak to me." His young voice raised. "You just don't know!"

Kay nodded.

"I've never experienced anything quite like that myself," she said. "But I'm sure I do know what it's like. I'm sure it's very hard for you."

"It's so tough I just can't go to school anymore."

"I was afraid that some of the kids in school wouldn't be particularly kind to you," she went on. "It's very unfortunate that they don't see the importance of trying to help you get straightened out and build a good reputation. That's no reason for you to stay away from school though."

"It is to me," Kent stormed.

"This situation won't last long," she said. "When they see that you're determined to live this down and to develop a good reputation, you'll find that they'll be nice to you again."

For a brief moment their eyes met.

"No, they won't," he said. "Oh, no, they won't!"

With that he dashed into his bedroom and slammed the door shut behind him.

When Danny came home later in the evening after a day of flying for the mission, the first thing he did was ask about Kent.

"I'm afraid the kids are giving him a rough time, Danny," Kay said, "especially at school. Very few of them will speak to him or have anything to do with him."

"I was afraid something like that would happen." Danny crossed to the big chair in the far corner of the living room and sat down. "People are strange. Very strange. They can know a fellow is a rascal and think he's still a great guy, as long as he isn't caught. But let the police arrest him and, boy, nobody will have anything to do with him."

Kay breathed deeply.

"I can't help feeling sorry for Kent, Danny. He acts as though he really wants to get straightened out, but the other kids don't want to let him."

"I feel sorry for him, too," her young husband said, "but if we're going to help him we've got to give him more than sympathy."

"If only he would yield his heart and his life to

Christ," Kay said pensively. "Then everything would be so different for him. He'd have something solid to build on."

"I know." He spoke softly. "But whenever I have tried to talk with him about the Lord it seems as though he freezes up inside."

Kay nodded. "The same thing happens when I try to talk with him."

"To tell you the truth," Danny went on, "I've never been able to find even a spark of interest. He doesn't seem to want to have anything to do with God. As long as he feels that way, I'm afraid there isn't very much we can do for him."

"I know you're right," Kay said, "but that doesn't make it any easier for me to see him the way he is."

"Nor for me."

After a time Kay spoke again.

"Danny, let's have a time of prayer for Kent. God is the only one who can straighten out the mess he's made of his life."

Together they knelt beside the divan. As they prayed, a certain peace came over them. When Danny got to his feet some minutes later he was smiling.

"Kay," he said softly, "I know God is going to answer our prayers for Kent. I don't know how long we will have to wait, or what it will take to bring him through for Christ, *but I know it's going to take place!*"